Hilda Hopkins
The Early Years

Volumes 1-3 Comprising

'Hilda Hopkins, Murder, She Knit'
'Hilda Hopkins, Bed & Burial'
'Hilda Hopkins, Domi Knit Rix'

Vivienne Fagan

StreetWise Publications

Published by StreetWise Publications
Suite 1/22 Waikanda Cres, Whalan, NSW 2770
Australia
All Rights Reserved.
http://streetwiseworldpublications.info

'Hilda Hopkins, Murder, She Knit' first published 2011
'Hilda Hopkins, Bed & Burial' first published 2011
'Hilda Hopkins, Domi Knit Rix' first published 2011

This Three Volume Compendium edition first
published 2012
Copyright Vivienne Fagan 2011

Fagan, Vivienne 1948-

ISBN 978-1480122390

Disclaimer: This is a work of fiction. Any resemblance to any person, living or dead, is coincidental and unintentional. The publisher, author and their officers and assigns assume no responsibility for the misuse of wool or knitting machines. No yarn was harmed in the writing of this story.

Hilda Hopkins, Murder, She Knit

Vivienne Fagan

Dedication

With grateful thanks to Kevin and Jamie-Lee for their advice regarding Police Procedure.

Prologue

"There's three of the things in here, Sir" called out Police Constable Clive Barcroft, opening the door of a display cabinet in the corner of the sitting room. He glanced at a paper in his hand and compared the photographs shown there with the finely detailed faces of three knitted dolls who stood smartly to attention, held in place by doll stands.

"Looks like Morris, Johnson and Bartlett, Sir. You know what, she's bloody good."

The elderly woman sitting in the kitchen looked up as she heard the young constable's comments. She smiled serenely and nodded.

"There are another two in the front parlour," added DS Claire Naylor, "either side of the mantelpiece."

"That will be Mr Abbott and Mr Tompkins," murmured the old lady, "and you'll find Mr Smith in my bedroom, on top of the bookcase, next to Abigail. Of course I didn't make Abigail," she continued vaguely, "men are much easier, they are craggier in the face and there's not so much shaping, perhaps the odd beer belly but one doesn't have to worry about the size of the bra cups."

The police woman who was standing behind the old lady's chair looked baffled. Was the old dear senile, and wandering in her mind?

Detective Inspector John Brent however had no such illusions.

"So where have you hidden them all, Mrs Hopkins?" he asked gently, "we've found two in the coal cellar, and the one in the lock, where did you put the others?"

Barcroft had appeared holding the three dolls in his arms. They were each about eighteen inches high, beautifully crafted with startlingly life like faces.

"Oh, my little gentlemen," crooned Hilda Hopkins, "you mustn't take them away, they belong here." She stood up. "I need to go to the toilet," she announced, making for the door. "You'll find Mr Abbott and Mr Tompkins behind the shed in the garden. They are not very deep, I just can't handle a spade now like I used to."

She smiled benignly and headed towards the downstairs cloakroom as Brent moved towards the back door.

"Leave those things on the table, Constable" he told Barcroft, "and come with me."

Claire Naylor hurried through from the front parlour and dropped two more dolls onto the table before following the men outside. The remaining officer, Barbara Grey examined the dolls as she watched the door of the cloakroom. They were all roughly the same height, but there the similarity ended. Each one had his own face and hair style. Barbara picked up the sheet of photographs of missing persons which Barcroft had laid on the table. The faces were very easy to identify. How had she done it? Some of the features had been formed by knitting in a contrast yarn, other details had been highlighted by the use of a fine permanent maker and fabric paints. Two of the dolls wore glasses, tiny little doll spectacles in perfect proportion to their faces. The clothes too were carefully crafted to suit each character, and fitted each doll perfectly.

Barbara glanced towards the cloakroom door. The old lady had been in there some time, she hoped she hadn't passed out or anything. Eventually she crossed over and rapped on the door panels.

"Are you all right Mrs Hopkins," she called.

There was no answer. Barbara stood there, unsure what to do. She rattled the doorknob but the door was locked. Concerned now, she decided to go round the house and try to look in through the window. To think was to act, and she let herself out of the front door. The cloakroom window was opened to its fullest extent, the cloakroom itself was empty. How on earth had a woman of that age climbed out of the window? And more importantly, where was she now?

PC Grey ran to the front gate and looked up and down Merrydown Crescent, nothing. Surely she couldn't have gone through the back garden, not with all those police officers swarming all over it. She'd have to tell DI Brent that she had lost her. She'd lost the suspect, a woman who was alleged to have done away with six elderly men. He was not going to be best pleased.

Chapter 1

Hilda Hopkins sat in the corner of a café in Midchester and pensively stirred her cup of tea. She'd been lucky when she had left the house after scrambling through the window. She'd slipped down Merrydown Crescent and turned the corner just as the Midchester bus trundled along the main road. She'd had her bus pass in her cardigan pocket along with a small wallet of credit cards. Once arrived in Midchester, the neighbouring town to her own small village, Hilda had quickly cleared the dead men's accounts of all their remaining money. Serves them right, she had thought, if the Banks or the Police hadn't got round to closing the accounts yet, what did they expect? She could put the money to good use.

She wasn't really hungry yet, the excitement of the morning had robbed her of her appetite. The appearance at her door of a senior police officer and his team had been something of a shock. She wondered how they had got on to her. She took a sip of tea. Well, she'd think about that later, she'd have a slap up meal in a good restaurant and consider the problem fully. In the meantime she needed to find somewhere to rest. She finished the tea, paid up and left.

Along the road were two or three charity shops. Hilda wandered into the first one and bought herself a slightly battered looking suitcase on wheels. The next shop provided her with a serviceable, if dowdy coat and woolly hat, together with a slightly shabby but good quality tweed skirt, a couple of blouses and a woolen jumper. She wrinkled her nose over the jumper. A bought one, how long was it since she had actually bought a jumper? She much preferred to make her own on her trusty knitting machine. Still, needs must when the devil drives. Underwear next, but not from here though, Hilda did have a touch of fastidiousness about her, there was an M&S further along the High Street, they would have nighties too.

Everything fitted neatly into her suitcase. Hilda donned the hat and coat, and pottered along the road looking every inch the suburban pensioner intent on an afternoon's shopping. She entered the portals of a Journey Lodge and approached the counter. It took several minutes for the young woman at Reception to notice her. Hilda felt the old stirrings of resentment. No-one ever took any notice of her, she might as well be invisible. She paid for a room for two nights with cash, filling out the forms with the name and address of one of her neighbours. She was handed the key, directed to the lift, and otherwise ignored.

Back at 46 Merrydown Crescent, Barbara Grey surreptitiously wiped her eyes dry. DI Brent had been furious, and had wasted no words in his opinion of someone who could lose an elderly woman in a tiny under stairs cloakroom. Clive Barcroft gave her a sympathetic grin as they returned to their patrol car preparatory to hunting for the woman. John Brent was a good bloke to work for, but he did have a rough edge to his tongue if he considered the occasion demanded it. Scenes of crime tape festooned the neat suburban garden, and a tent had been erected to cover the excavations behind the shed.

"Well at least she hasn't actually been arrested yet, Barb," said Barcroft sympathetically, "if she'd already been charged with all those murders the shit really would have hit the fan."

Barbara Grey shuddered, "I know, thirteen days' pay docked and a Final Warning letter, my career wouldn't have survived that, Clive."

"Let's get on with it," he murmured, "the old dear couldn't have gone far."

"She's gone far enough to get me one hell of a bollocking," replied Grey resentfully, "I really want to track her down Clive, and snap a pair of cuffs onto her wrists. She won't bolt a second time."

They had reached the end of Merrydown Crescent, Barcroft paused to let a bus go past. Grey read the destination board, "Midchester Town Centre".

"She might have caught that bus, or rather another one going to Midchester. It's a fair sized place, she could lose herself there to some extent. Did you see her Clive? Whoever would have thought she would be capable of anything like this, let alone carry it out. Do you think anyone helped her? She looks like a fat Miss Marple."

"Except the Marple woman is always on the right side of the law," replied Barcroft.

"She lured six old men into her house as lodgers….."

"Paying guests" interrupted Barcroft, "remember she said her gentlemen had been there as paying guests."

"Whatever," snapped Grey, "and then she did away with them. Wonder what the post mortems will show, poison do you reckon?"

"Well it is a women's thing, generally, poison," Barcroft reflected, "but it's those doll effigies that spook me. Did you see them?"

Grey nodded. She had been examining them when Mrs Hopkins had scrambled out of the window and made her escape.

"They are very clever," she acknowledged. "Why do you reckon she made them? Some sort of trophy?"

Barcroft shrugged his shoulders,

"I've no idea."

They drove in silence for some time before entering the environs of Midchester. Barcroft drove slowly along the High Street while Grey craned her neck and inspected every grey haired old lady, and there were a lot of them about at this time of the day. They circumnavigated the town, criss-crossing the streets but there was no sign of their quarry.

"Either gone to ground, or not here at all," decided Barcroft. "We'd better get back."

Chapter 2

Hilda returned to her hotel room from the restaurant where she had treated herself to the promised slap up meal. She settled in an armchair and turned on the local news. She was the first item.

"Police are concerned about the whereabouts of Hilda Hopkins," here a photograph flashed onto the screen. "They wish to speak to her regarding some irregularities concerning lodgers who resided in her house."

"Paying guests, not lodgers," fumed Hilda, who was nonetheless pleased with the photograph they had used. It was a copy of her bus pass photo, taken when she was still colouring her hair a rich brown. Now it was snow white, and her skin, which had been of the famous English peaches and cream variety, had, over the past few months, crumpled into wrinkles like a dried out apple. She bore little resemblance now to the smooth skinned dark haired individual in the photograph. She would be able to fade into the background for a little while longer.

There had been a brief view of the house, neatly roped off with blue police tape, and a hint of the activity still going on in the back garden. She would go to prison when she was caught of course. She was realistic enough to appreciate that, but she wondered if they would let her keep the dolls, her little gentlemen. Would they have craft classes or clubs in prison? Maybe if she got a long sentence she would be able to have her knitting machine sent in. She would like that, machine knitting was her passion.

She giggled to herself. What would she give to see the smug faces of her neighbours and her ex work colleagues when they found out what she had been doing. Would they believe she was capable of carrying all that out on her own? They hadn't found Mr Smith yet by all accounts. Mr Bartlett and Mr Morris had been in the coal cellar. She was rather glad they had been discovered because truth to tell, they had been starting to smell. Nothing too obtrusive just yet, just a lingering miasma in the air, but it certainly wouldn't have improved with time.

Mr Abbott and Mr Tompkins were behind the shed in the garden. That had been hard work even though they were in shallow graves. She had scattered the loose earth over the rest of the garden, but there had been so much of it! That was why she had dumped Mr Johnson in the canal lock just beyond the end of her garden. She had had to leave him in the shed for a day, he was much too heavy to drag all the way there in one go. All her gentlemen had been of slight build in life, but goodness, they had been so heavy once they were dead.

Maybe she could say that Mr Smith had killed the others, and had disappeared once he knew the old bill were on his track. She could make out she had been his unwilling accomplice, too scared to resist. That might be a bit difficult though, Mr Smith had disappeared from her house long before Mr Bartlett and Mr Morris the two men who had each ended up in the coal cellar, had arrived. She should have thought of that sooner, stayed in the house and passed herself off as a frightened vulnerable old lady. Running away would simply complicate matters, unless of course she had believed that Mr Smith was going to take her away from all this? She could say he was supposed to meet her, but he hadn't turned up. It wouldn't be the first time she had been dumped. Mr Hopkins had walked out on her less than six months into their marriage.

"Just popping out to get some fags, love," he had said, "won't be long."

That had been well over thirty years ago and he still hadn't found his way back home. Not even when her widowed mother had died and Hilda had inherited the three bedroomed semi, so much nicer than the furnished flat she had been renting.

She would have an early night, and go for a leisurely breakfast in the morning. What a pity she hadn't thought to buy a book to read in the charity shop.

Hilda changed into her nightdress, and settled herself on the bed. It had been a tiring day. She drifted half in and out of sleep, mulling over the events of the past three years.

Chapter 3

Hilda had retired after thirty odd undistinguished years of Local Government service. She hadn't managed to save much over the years, it seemed to her that everything she earned went on the nitty gritty of living. Plus of course she had her hobby, she was an ardent machine knitter. Over the years she had collected every magazine and book about machine knitting that she could find. She had also spent large amounts of money on yarn and equipment. So once she stopped working and found herself existing on a small pension she found that she really did need a second income. She briefly considered selling the jumpers and other bits and pieces that she made on her machine, but there wasn't much call for that sort of thing these days. Machine knitting had had its heyday, it was a craft only followed now by a small but enthusiastic number of committed adherents.

Hilda thought about the layout of her house. She had changed the box room into a small knitting room, and she herself slept in the back bedroom. It was a little smaller than the master bedroom, but it was away from the road so a bit quieter. Not that there was much traffic passing around Merrydown Crescent. She decided that she could let the larger bedroom out and earn some money from the rent.

She had deliberated long and hard about what sort of person to have as a lodger. Certainly not a student, another woman perhaps? But Hilda didn't really get on too well with other women. She had made no lasting friends at work, and she had been asked to leave her knitting club for constantly causing upset there. They had just been jealous of her of course, she thought bitterly, she had been much cleverer at making things than the others. They had tried to say her knitting tensions were wrong, her knitting was too loose, it needed to be tighter for well-fitting cuffs and welts, and that Emmie woman had said that her mattress stitch wasn't even. Hers wasn't any better in Hilda's opinion, and she had had no compunction in saying so. Naturally the stupid woman had burst into tears, and the Club leader had suggested that Hilda might like to find another club. Hilda knew that she had been better than any of them. It was the same old story, people were always envious of her because she was far superior than any of them.

So, a male lodger. No, a paying guest. That sounded much better. Someone with a bit of age and dignity, no riff raff. A professional man. But then, wouldn't a professional man already have his own home, would there be any who would just want a room? She had worried round the problem like a terrier gnawing at a bone. In the end she decided she would see who actually replied to her advertisement in the newsagents' window in Midchester. There'd been no point advertising locally, she knew there were no spare men looking for accommodation in her village. They would have to share the bathroom with her, but she would make out a rota, some sort of timetable so they wouldn't both be trying to get in there at the same time. She would cook the meals and they could eat at the kitchen table and the guest would have the use of the sitting room, but the front parlour was going to be private for her. She would just have to see who would turn up.

What turned up was Mr Arthur Smith. Sixty-six years old, widowed, childless and sick and tired of living on the fourth floor of a building with no lift. He was a small slight man, very nearly totally bald, and very quietly spoken. Hilda found him eminently suitable. He liked his bed room, and was quite content to sit in the sitting room all day watching television. He ate the meals which Hilda put in front of him. She wasn't a particularly good cook, although of course she believed that each meal she produced had a touch of haute cuisine about it, and Arthur Smith was canny enough to thank her gravely each day for his meals. He was a man who liked a quiet life, and he could read something in Hilda's face which warned him not to upset her.

He had been staying at Hilda's house for nearly six months when he was late down for his breakfast one morning. Hilda slid two hard fried eggs onto a cold plate, added a dollop of baked beans, and fished two rashers of streaky bacon from under the grill where they were rapidly turning black round the edges. Hilda laid the plate on the table and went to the kitchen door. There was no sound at all from upstairs. Sighing she ascended the stairs and rapped on the bedroom door.

"Breakfast is on the table Mr Smith."

No answer.

"It's going to get cold. Are you up yet?"

No answer.

Knock, knock, knock.

No answer.

Hilda had taken five months' rent off Mr Smith during his stay, she hoped he hadn't done a moonlight flit leaving her short of this month's rent. Tentatively she opened the door and peeped inside.

Arthur Smith lay on the narrow single bed. He was deathly pale, deathly still, deathly cold. Hilda moved across to the bed and briefly touched his forehead, it was icy cold. She let out an involuntary squeak and retreated to the landing. What now? She supposed she would have to ring 999. Who would be responsible for his funeral? Did he have enough money of his own to cover the cost? It was a pity she hadn't opened a life insurance policy on him….the thought popped unbidden into her head.

Hilda went back into the bedroom and looked down at Mr Smith. In life he had been a short, slight man, in death he appeared even smaller and more shrunken. His wallet lay on the bedside cabinet next to the bed. Hilda picked it up and rummaged through it. She would take the rent he owed her, even if he wasn't going to be here for the rest of the month. There were several currency notes, and a couple of bank and credit cards. There was also a small piece of paper, neatly folded. Curious, Hilda unfolded it, and discovered three sets of four figure numbers neatly written in Mr Smith's handwriting. Hilda realised that these must be the pin numbers for the cards.

She went downstairs and looked at the telephone. She made no move to pick up the receiver but instead went into the kitchen and poured the rapidly congealing breakfast into the waste bin. Calmly she made herself a cup of tea, and sat down to think. Mr Smith had had no visitors during the time he had lived in her house. Any mail that arrived for him was of a business rather than a personal nature. Would he be missed? She thought not. If she could park him somewhere out of sight and out of mind, she could relet the room. His pensions went into his bank account, he had never gone down to the Post Office to collect any benefits so he wasn't known there, and she had the pin numbers for all his cards. If she wasn't greedy she could withdraw a little each week, so long as the accounts were active and not in the red, surely no-one would notice.

Where to put him? He couldn't stay upstairs, especially if she was going to get another paying guest. She had a small garden to the front of the property, and a larger one behind. There was a gate at the end of the back garden which led out onto the tow path which ran alongside the canal. She considered the geography of the area. It could be done.

Hilda removed her slippers and put on her outdoor shoes. She went out into the back garden. Her stomach was churning with excitement. She could do this. If she had a steady income from Mr Smith's account would she even need another paying guest? She decided she had better get another one, just in case the neighbours noticed that Mr Smith wasn't around. They tended to be a nosey lot around here. She would choose someone similar, elderly and on the short side. People didn't bother looking too closely, one elderly chap coming-out her house would look much the same as any other at a cursory glance.

Hilda smiled, she hadn't had so much fun in years. But this plotting and scheming, it just showed what a clever woman she was. She had been passed over for promotion time and time again when she had been working. She knew why, they were jealous of her, scared for their own jobs because they knew if she got a toehold on the ladder she would be better than all of them and their jobs would be in danger. And then she had got older, so all the young ones got the advancement. What did they know about the work, they didn't have her experience. She had always obeyed the rules, never deviated, never took any short cuts just stuck to the book at all times, well, this was different. Now she would show them she could use her initiative. Or rather she wouldn't show them, she would do this under the noses of the neighbours and any one else who might show an interest, and get away with it. She would prove to them who was the best.

She let herself out of the garden gate, and looked up and down the tow path. About a hundred yards up the towpath there was a lock, the water churning at the foot of its gates. She started to walk downstream away from it. The houses curved away from the canal at this point, and the trees in the adjoining park came down to fringe the tow path. Hilda plunged in amongst the trees. She didn't want to have to drag the body too far, but it did need to be somewhere where it wouldn't be found too quickly either. There was a natural hollow amongst the roots of a tree which had been blown down during the winter storms. Hilda reckoned if she brought a spade along, she could deepen the hole slightly and Mr Smith would fit in there perfectly. She stirred the soil with her foot. It was quite loose. She glanced around. The hollow was far enough from the tow path not to be seen. It wasn't on the route of the dog walkers either, it could work. Hilda hurried back to her home, and took the spade from the garden shed. She wrapped it in a piece of sacking and scuttled back down the tow path to her chosen site. She had been right, the soil was fairly loose, and she was able to make a decent sized cave like hole under the tree. She left the spade there, wrapped in its piece of sacking; she would need it later to do some filling in.

The danger period would be getting him from the garden to the burial site. It was quiet enough now, but later on there would be joggers and dog walkers and goodness knew who else wandering along here. Hilda decided that she would wait until after dark that evening. She thought she would be able to find her way back to the tree easily enough; she had spotted a couple of landmarks she could use. She needed to get back to the shed. There was a wheel barrow in there she could use to transport the body, but it might need oiling. She didn't want to go creaking along the path calling attention to herself.

It had been a lot more difficult than she anticipated, but Hilda managed it. Once she had an idea, she was quite tenacious. She was amazed how heavy Mr Smith was as she struggled to manoeuvre his body down the stairs into the hall where she wrapped him in wheelie bin bags, tying string round and round his body to keep them in place before strapping him onto the wheelbarrow. Rigor had passed by now, and he flopped alarmingly as she balanced him on it. The oiling had worked well though, and she glided through the garden and along the path with the minimum of noise. He fitted quite nicely into the hole she had dug, and she soon had his body well covered in soil, followed by detritus and leaves which camouflaged the grave perfectly.

Hilda was exhausted, but curiously elated. She had done it. That would teach him to go and die on her. Now she would enjoy herself at his expense, literally. She giggled. She looked down at the ground, carefully flashing a torch around to make sure there was no hint of what was buried here. The smile left her face as she contemplated the grave. There could be no memorial, no headstone, no cross, that bothered her slightly. Her face creased in concern for a few minutes as she stood there in a contemplative silence. Her expression cleared, she knew what she would do. She would make one of her look a like dolls. Over the years Hilda had perfected her technique in making amazingly life like dolls. She made them to represent people at work who had annoyed her, either with a real or an imagined slight. She would take the dolls out and berate them, saying all the things she couldn't say to her colleagues for fear of losing her job. Some had even been slapped, or had arms and legs twisted as a punishment.

This one would be different though. She would keep the woolly Mr Smith in her bedroom as a tribute to his memory. He could stand on top of the wardrobe, next to Abigail, a porcelain doll which she had owned for years. She had his picture on his bus pass...yes, that would make a fitting memorial, combining her interests and skill with his demise. Hilda turned-on her heel and returned to the house, eager to start designing her little gentleman doll.

Chapter 4

Hilda woke early the next morning, and stretched luxuriously in the comfortable double bed. She opened her eyes and had a moment of confusion as the unfamiliar room met her gaze. Then she remembered, she was a fugitive from the law. How exciting, Hilda Hopkins, armed and dangerous! Well not armed, but she had nothing to lose now if anyone crossed her. She giggled as she threw back the covers and went into the bathroom. The shower was lovely. It was a power one, and quite fierce. Hilda stood under the jets of water and felt the force of the water on her skin. It was exhilarating. She would dry herself, dress and go down for an early breakfast.

She finished drying her hair and replaced the hairdryer neatly in the fitment drawer. Today she would wear the skirt and jumper she had bought in the charity shop. They weren't all that appealing, but the police had a description of what she had been wearing yesterday. She dressed herself and went across to open the curtains. Her window overlooked the entrance to the car park. As she jerked the curtains aside, she looked down to see a police car driving into the forecourt. She leapt back from the window, heart pounding and sat on the edge of the bed. Were they looking for her? The chances were quite high. And when she had booked in she had used the name and address of a neighbour just along the Crescent from her. It had seemed amusing at the time, but perhaps she should have used a purely fictional address. The police would zoom in on that, they weren't stupid, and they must have some idea what they were dealing with now.

Hilda picked up the carrier bag which had contained her new underwear. Quickly she stuffed one spare pair of pants and a bra in there, she would just have to wash a change of underwear each day once she was settled somewhere. She added the two blouses she had bought yesterday to the bag. She slipped her money and bus pass into the pocket of the dowdy brown coat along with the woolly hat. She glanced around the room. Yesterday's skirt, blouse and cardigan lay over the armchair, her nightdress was on the bed. She would leave her toiletries in the bathroom too, so it would look as if she had popped out for breakfast and intended returning. She picked up the carrier bag and let herself out of the room. It had taken minutes. She walked along the corridor to the lift, then paused. She might meet the police officers in the lobby if she went this way. There was a flight of service stairs at the end of the corridor, she went down those and let herself out round the side of the car park. She headed towards the low wall surrounding the building, sat on the parapet, and with a surprising show of grace, swung her legs over the top of the wall and onto the pavement.

Breakfast. That needed to be the first priority. If she was well fed she could concentrate on the day ahead. Hilda ambled along the road, trying to appear unconcerned and succeeded completely. No-one took any notice of her whatsoever. She came across a small café, a "greasy spoon" and decided this would do. She paid for a full breakfast and was pleasantly surprised when it arrived. The bacon and sausage were nicely cooked, as were the mushrooms and black pudding, the fried egg was runny, the toast a pleasing brown and they hadn't been stingy with the butter either. The cup of tea was a disappointment. It had been poured out of a large metal teapot, and Hilda reckoned they must make one pot in the morning and fill it up with more hot water and the odd extra spoonful of tea as the morning went on. It tasted stewed and was far too strong. Still, she needed to keep a low profile so she bit back her natural desire to complain and got on with the meal.

Where to now, she wondered. If the police had come as far as Midchester searching for her, they probably had the bus station and the railway station alerted too. She didn't drive. She briefly considered buying, or even stealing a bicycle but it was years since she had ridden one. She left the café and wandered through the streets with no particular destination in mind. She came across the canal. It was the same one that ran behind her house. A little further along she could see a small jetty. A barge was moored there next to a sign proclaiming "Canal Trips. Three hours duration." A blackboard next to the sign announced that the next trip would be at 11am. Hilda checked the time, it was nearly a quarter to ten. With a bit of luck the police would be relying on her returning to her room in the Journey Lodge. After all her possessions were there and she had paid for two nights. She felt that she would be safe pottering around the High Street amongst the other elderly shoppers until she could return here and buy a ticket for the canal trip. Once they arrived at the destination, she would quietly disappear, and they could return without her. She had been on the odd canal trip before years ago, and she knew that sometimes people caught a later barge back if they wanted to sightsee for more than the fifteen minutes stay.

It all worked out as she had planned. Of course it had, she thought self-righteously as she settled herself in her seat, she was organising it, there was no way it could go wrong. Hadn't she proved herself to be the best so far? Twice now she had out-witted the police.

It was a pleasant trip. The barge glided along between the fields and Hilda felt herself relax. She mustn't get complacent though, she reminded herself. She had to keep her wits about her if she was to stay free. The barge gently bumped into its mooring, and Hilda accepted the hand of the young bargeman to assist her back onto dry land.

They had arrived at the small village of Neston. The young man had helped several other passengers off the barge, and obligingly pointed to a passage just ahead of them.

"If you go through there, you'll be in the High Street, There's a couple of nice tea rooms, and if you like gardens, you can walk along to Neston House and see the gardens there for free. You can go round the house too, but you have to pay for that. We're leaving on the half hour, but we'll be back an hour after that if you want to stay longer."

Hilda grinned. They obviously didn't check who got on or off their barge. If you missed the last one, tough, you'd have to find your own back to Midchester. Well that suited her fine. She didn't want a hue and cry because they had lost a passenger. She tagged along behind the knot of people heading towards the village. A cup of tea would be nice, and perhaps a toasted tea cake, dripping with butter to accompany it? Hilda was starting to appreciate the finer things of life now that there was a strong chance they would be snatched away from her. She didn't suppose that toasted tea cakes would appear on a prison menu.

As she emerged from the passage, Hilda noticed a queue composed mainly of women outside a hall halfway down the road. Curious she strolled towards them. There was a large poster on the side of the wall, "Jumble Sale, Neston Village Hall, Saturday, 11am (this had been crossed out and 12 noon scribbled in its place) tea and refreshments, admission 20p." Hilda liked jumble sales at the best of times, and serendipitously she had arrived in good time to visit this one. She fumbled in her pocket, fished out 20p and joined the end of the queue just as the doors opened and the crowd surged forward.

The first stall inside the hall was covered in bags and shoes. To one side Hilda spotted a blue and green tartan shopping trolley on wheels. She snatched it up and waved it at the helper behind the table.

`"50p, dear."

Armed with her trolley Hilda turned her attention to the rest of the jumble sale. She thoroughly enjoyed herself. She loved being in the scrum, fighting over a garment, diving forward to pick up a book before another hand grasped it. She bought herself another skirt, a jacket, and a pair of trousers, plus a couple of blouses, a head scarf and several books. Everything went into the shopping trolley. It was a nice one, sturdily built with solid rubber tyres on large wheels. It would be very useful.

Hilda looked over at the refreshments. She read the list, tea, coffee, cold drinks and digestive biscuits. Tea would be fine, but she had a real hankering for a toasted tea cake. She decided to go in search of a proper tea room. As she was manoeuvring the trolley down the steps of the village hall a police car drove past. Hilda had her head averted as she bumped the trolley down, and the car passed without slowing down and continued on its way out of the village.

Hilda stood gazing after it. She was so clever. They couldn't even catch her when she was within feet of them. Complacently she towed her new shopping trolley behind her and strolled down the road. The Willow Tree Tea Room proved to be delightful. Hilda sat by the window, there was tea in a real teapot, a china cup and saucer had been placed in front of her, and milk appeared in its own matching jug. Hilda poured out her first cup, and sat there in seventh heaven savouring the exquisite flavour. How very different from the café where she had breakfasted! The waitress appeared bearing a plate on which not one, but two toasted teacakes nestled. They were delicious, plump, nicely toasted, bursting with fruit and slathered in butter. Real butter, not a cheap spread. This was luxury indeed.

Mr Bartlett would have liked this, she reflected. She frowned. He had been such a fussy eater. He had dared to criticise her cooking, and she could cook, like everything else she did, she was excellent at it, or so she believed. Mr Bartlett had been Mr Smith's successor. He too had been elderly, a slight man with no family or friends that Hilda could discover. She had interviewed several people for the room before she had decided on him. He was in his seventies and looked very frail, hopefully he would go the same way as Mr Smith. But he was such a complainer! Mr Smith hadn't worried about hard fried eggs; Mr Bartlett told her he could only eat eggs if they were runny, and would she please warm the plates because his meals got cold so quickly.

He had a habit of looking at the plateful of food and curling his lip back, ever so slightly. This really infuriated Hilda. One day he told her that he didn't fancy chicken, he had gone off it, would she kindly provide something different for him in future, please? Hilda bought chicken a lot. Not only did she enjoy eating it, it was cheap and plentiful. She tried buying TV meals which she heated up in the oven for Mr Bartlett. He wasn't keen on these either, he said they were too dry and they all tasted the same. How could they taste the same she had fumed silently to herself when they were all different varieties? Why wouldn't the infuriating man just quietly expire in the middle of the night the same as the obliging Mr Smith?

One morning he came into the kitchen a little early. Hilda was making scrambled eggs. The mixture wasn't setting properly. She had the gas turned up beneath the pan as she stirred the eggs and milk, but it obstinately retained its fluidity. She was starting to lose her temper. Her face suffused to a dark red, small flecks of spittle collected on her lips and she banged the top edges of the pan with the spoon, making small dents around the edge.

"At my last place," commented Mr Bartlett, settling himself at the table and opening his newspaper, "we always had scrambled eggs made in the microwave. Lovely they were, always creamy. Handy things microwaves Mrs Hopkins, you don't seem to have one?"

"I'm not having one of those things in here," snapped Hilda, "they're dangerous, waves can leak out of them and give you tumours, I've read about it."

The egg mixture in the pan turned suddenly from liquid to a solid mass. She mashed it up with a fork and piled it onto a couple of slices of leathery toast.

"You might need to put some butter on that," she said, pushing a tub of vegetable spread across the table.

"I've never heard of that before," commented Mr Bartlett.

Hilda gazed at him before she realised he was talking about microwave ovens and not buttery scrambled eggs.

"I've no time for new fangled things like that. I've got my food processor and a blender, that's enough gadgets for me to be going on with. I don't want anything nasty leaking out in my kitchen."

"They are quite safe, you know, these days," continued Mr Bartlett as if Hilda hadn't spoken, "and you can use them for all sorts of things, microwave meals, defrosting stuff, nice scrambled eggs."

He had eaten half of his egg on toast, and pushed the remainder away with an expression of distaste.

Hilda pursed her lips. This one was too healthy to pop his clogs in the middle of the night, he might need a bit of help to shuffle off this mortal coil. Nothing too messy. Hilda was an avid fan of CSI, she knew a lot about blood splatter and luminal. There were fingerprints and DNA to take into account too. Committing the perfect crime was much harder these days, but of course if you were as clever as Hilda believed herself to be, it was just a matter of a little forward planning.

What about poison? Hilda had thought long and hard about that, but where would she get poison from? It had been all right in Victorian times, arsenic could be found all around the house, it was used in so many things, but in these days of Health and Safety there were too many restrictions. Antifreeze was supposed to be pretty lethal, but it would look odd if she bought that down at the local garage seeing that she didn't drive or own a motor vehicle. There was rat poison too, but did she want the man in the shop thinking she had vermin in her spotless house? She thought not. Plus it needed to be quick, she didn't want to see her gentleman suffering, even if he had turned his nose up at her cooking. She wasn't a nurse, she couldn't cope with a long illness. Hilda herself had very robust health and despised bodily weakness in others.

It was two separate television programmes which finally solved the problem for her. One was fictional, the other a documentary. In the fictional story the baddie had sedated her victims with valerian before despatching them. The other was a documentary programme dealing with the history of the garrotte. Hilda reflected that if she used both things together, the valerian to sedate her gentleman, then the garrotte to finish him off, it would be a clean kill. Plus she wouldn't have to see his face as she did it either, Hilda was a little squeamish about some things. She could knit a garrotte, and use a knitting needle to wind it tight.... It would work....what a clever and resourceful woman she was, and what a shame she couldn't proclaim that from the rooftops!

First of all though, she needed to be sure that she had her facts right. She trotted off down Merrydown Crescent and caught the bus into Midchester. She knew there was a herbal shop in the precinct there. On the pretence that she suffered badly from insomnia, Hilda closely questioned the shop's owner about sleeping draughts. He actually suggested Valerian tablets, warning her not to drive if she took them as they were quite potent. Hilda thanked him profusely, with an effort she could appear quite gracious. She dithered and twittered a little as she imagined old people must do, and asked if she could buy several bottles to save her the journey into town, it was such an ordeal at her age, especially if she didn't get a seat on the bus. The man, kindness itself, not only wrapped up several bottles for her, but even gave her a discount for bulk.

Hilda spent some time experimenting with different weights and types of yarn. She knitted long cords, then practised the strangulation on a baby doll. She kept this as a model for displaying the baby clothes she sometimes made. Some of the cords gave too much, and she decided she would have to make them using a much firmer tension. After several abortive attempts she settled on a wool and nylon mix. The wool was soft to the touch, it would be gentle on the old man's neck, and the nylon added strength. It wouldn't do for the cord to stretch or break when it was being used for real.

Hilda sat on the edge of her bed, the baby doll on her knee, twisting the knitting needle round and round, before deciding that a double pointed thicker needle would be better. The thinner ones tended to bend as the knot tightened. The baby doll lay limply across her knee, there were Herod genes somewhere in Hilda's make up.

All her preparations paid off. Mr Bartlett drank his well laced coffee, and actually fell asleep at the table, falling across his plate. Hilda slipped the loop of brown wool over his head, poked the knitting needle through the cord, then twisted and twisted, pulling Mr Bartlett's head up from the table as she struggled to make the cord tighter. It bit into the old man's neck, cutting off the circulation. Mr Bartlett's arms and legs twitched feebly, and then it was done. His body slumped to one side, and Hilda was nearly pulled off balance as he slid towards the floor. She hauled up on the cord and straightened him out. Tentatively she let the cord slacken. She pulled the needle out of it and watched fascinated as the twisted cord folded in on itself. Would she leave it on him? It might be used as evidence some time in the future if she was very unlucky and got caught. And it would be bad luck, she was far too clever to be caught out by carelessness, but you could never depend on luck, it was fickle, it could be good or bad. She reckoned she had better remove the cord while she could.

Blood splatter; she would have to be careful and make sure she didn't cut him. Did dead men bleed? She couldn't remember, better be safe than sorry. Hilda fetched her thinnest, sharpest pair of scissors from her work room and returned to the corpse. She gingerly inserted the scissors' blade under the cord and snipped away it. She eased it free of his neck, sliding it along gently before dropping it in the bin. The bin men came on Tuesday that would soon be long gone in the landfill.

She already had the wheelie bin bags ready. This time she would use duct tape to tie it all up. She had used string on Mr Smith and it had slipped about something chronic. Still she wasn't taking Mr Bartlett as far as Mr Smith. She would use the old coal cellar outside the back door. It had been disused since central heating had been installed in the house. It was more of an outhouse than an actual cellar, but the door was always kept locked, and there was still a pile of coal in there at the very back. Hilda hauled Mr Bartlett over the coals (in a manner of speaking) and settled him in the far corner, covering his body with the small black rocks until nothing more could be seen.

She went up to his room and neatly packed all his belongings away. They could go up in the loft with Mr Smith's things. She removed the money from his wallet and hunted through his paper work until she found a small card with pin numbers written on the back. It seemed to be a common thing amongst the elderly, writing down their numbers so that memory loss wouldn't leave them destitute. The bed was stripped, all the bedding went into the washing machine, new newspaper lined the drawers, a quick Hoover round and a flick with the duster...perfect Hilda had thought, all ready for the next one......

"Have you finished?"

Hilda came out of her reverie and looked up at the waitress.

"It's just that we get busy on Saturday afternoons," explained the girl picking up Hilda's plate.

Hilda glanced round the tearoom, it was half empty, but she had been sitting there for some time. She was wearing that god awful coat too, the girl probably thought she was some sort of bag lady. She had had to leave her good cream woollen coat behind at the house, she could hardly have taken that into the loo with her. The policewoman certainly wouldn't have fallen for that. Still, she mustn't draw attention to herself even though she was itching to tell this insolent girl off for her cheek.

"Yes thank you. I'll have the bill, please."

Hilda paid up, leaving a meagre 10p tip, and wandered out into the main thoroughfare, towing her shopping trolley behind her. Where to now? She didn't want to go back to Midchester, but where could she spend the night? She turned off the main road and ambled down one side road and into another. This was a lovely street she thought, looking round at all the little bungalows set back behind high hedges. She pottered along, looking through the gates at the neat gardens. Ahead of her a van was drawn up partly onto the pavement. It was a supermarket delivery van. Hilda paused, debating whether to cross the road. She was getting tired, she really needed to sit down for a few minutes. There was a small pathway between two bungalows towards the back of the van. Hilda turned into it and walked down a few yards until she found a low wall she could sit on.

She heard the doors of the van slam, the engine started up, and it drew away and disappeared down the road. Hilda continued to sit on her perch. She turned her head as she heard voices coming from the other side of the hedge.

"I've put the perishables in the fridge, Sue" said a deep voice, "I completely forgot the shopping was due. I was so intent on surprising you."

"You're such a sweetie," presumably this was Sue. Hilda eased herself round slightly and tried to look through the hedge but it was too thick.

"It's just like you, Brian, to swing a surprise holiday on me! Put that last bag in the kitchen would you?"

There was a rustling sound as something was lifted and taken into the bungalow.

Voices sounded again just inside the open door of the bungalow. Hilda strained her ears, she had excellent hearing for her age. A useful asset for someone who was such a nosey parker.

"Well I thought five days in Venice would be a nice run up to our proper holiday," said Brian, "hurry up Sue, the taxi should be here in a couple of minutes. I think I've packed everything you'll need in your bag, I didn't want to spoil the surprise by asking you what you'd want to take. Anyway, anything you're missing we'll buy when we get there."

"I must look a mess," replied Susan, "you didn't give me chance to shower or anything."

"You look wonderful, as ever," replied Brian.

Hilda's mouth turned down at the corners. A wave of envy poured over her. Her husband hadn't treated her to surprise holidays, the only surprise he had ever sprung on Hilda was to disappear one afternoon.

The taxi arrived on cue.

"Have you got your passport?" called out Brian.

"In my handbag where it always lives," laughed Sue, "what about yours?"

"It's here safe with the tickets. I didn't let Mrs O'Grady know we were going away, we'll have to ring her once we get there."

"She's away for the week," said Sue, banging the door shut, "gone to Herne Bay to stay with her Colin and his wife and the grandchildren. Remember, I told you we'd have to clean for ourselves this week."

"Not now we won't. Shove that key under the pot Sue, just in case Mrs O'Grady gets back before us. Come on, the taxi's waiting, he'll have his clock on."

There was a flurry of footsteps, and much slamming of car doors. Hilda pressed back into the hedge as the taxi swept by, but there was little chance of her being seen.

She sat and waited for a good five minutes. There was no more traffic, no pedestrians, just silence. She went round to the gate and boldly walked up the path. She knew instinctively that furtive scurrying would call attention to herself, she had to look as if she belonged here. She examined the small flowerbed directly in front of the bungalow. An upturned flowerpot sat discreetly towards the back. Hilda peeped underneath and saw a Yale key. She snatched it up and inserted it into the lock, moments later she was inside the hall, the door closed behind her, heart thumping. This would make a glorious bolt hole for a few days while she worked out her next move.

Chapter 5

Detective Inspector John Brent looked round the room at the assembled officers and rapped on the desk for attention. All eyes swivelled towards him. He stood by a board on which were pinned several photographs and maps.

"We've retrieved the bodies of five men," he summarised, "a sixth is still missing, presumed dead. Preliminary findings from the pathologist indicate that the men were sedated then strangled. We've not identified the ligature that was used yet."

He looked irritably towards the back of the room where two uniformed officers sat near the door. The woman officer had muttered something to her colleague, who now had a broad grin on his face. Clive Barcroft felt Brent's eyes upon him, and hastily rearranged his face into a serious expression.

"Would you care to share your thoughts with us, Constable Grey," asked DI Brent frostily, "don't be coy Constable, let's hear your words of wisdom."

Barbara Grey flushed deeply crimson but answered steadily enough,

"I just wondered if she had knitted a noose to hang them with, Sir," she explained, "she had all sorts in that workroom of hers, a knitted clock, dolls all sorts. It seems to be something she's comfortable with, knitting I mean, and she seems to have quite an imagination………"

She trailed off as the senior officer gazed at her. She was already in his bad books having let Hopkins escape, was she digging a deeper hole to bury herself in?

"That Constable, is a very astute observation. Sergeant", Brent turned to Claire Naylor, "get on to Forensics and see if there were any fibres present on the wounds. If there are, we'll need to match them up with the yarn in the workroom. We'll get all of that bagged and labelled."

He swung back towards Barbara,

"Excellent, Constable. If you get any more bright ideas, share them with all of us not just your partner. This is a serious investigation and I welcome ideas from any of you."

He let his gaze travel over the group of officers,

"Don't be shy, I'll not bite your heads off. This woman has a natural cunning and the luck of the devil. We need to be as shrewd as she is. We nearly caught her this morning. Apparently she spent last night at the Journey Lodge in Midchester but she's disappeared again."

Barcroft nudged Barbara's arm and gave her a quick wink. She let out a sigh of relief. If only she could redeem herself further in the DI's estimation.

Chapter 6

Hilda left her shopping trolley in the hall while she examined her new quarters. The master bedroom was at the front of the bungalow, together with a smaller bedroom obviously used as a guest room. To the back was an even tinier room, Hilda reckoned it was smaller even than the box room she used as a workroom back in Melody Crescent. This room had been turned into a small office cum study. Hilda decided she would sleep in the spare bedroom, she wouldn't feel comfortable using the young couple's bed. The two comfortable looking single beds were already made up, it was ideal. The bathroom held a bath as well as a shower. Hilda inspected the range of toiletries in the cabinet. She would have a lovely long soak before bedtime.

The living room was at the rear of the bungalow, overlooking a long garden fringed by a high Leylandi hedge. Hilda pulled the heavy curtains across the windows, it was as well to be cautious she thought. She went through to the kitchen. The fridge was well stocked, plus there was a freezer and a cupboard full of tins and packets. There was also a microwave oven. Hilda looked at this askance and quickly pulled its plug out of the wall socket. She turned the kettle on, selected a mug from a cupboard and found the tea bags. She would make a nice cup of tea, and take the chance to relax before planning for the next stage of her escape.

Once she had finished her tea and washed the mug, Hilda went on a proper tour of inspection of the premises. She poked amongst the papers in the study. There was a state of the art computer sitting on a small desk next to a filing cabinet. Hilda turned it on. She was fairly competent with computers, she had a small home one which she used to keep track of goods on EBay, plus she belonged to a number of on-line knitting groups. She left the computer humming quietly to itself while she sorted through the drawers in the desk and the filing cabinet. Her search turned up a credit card in the name of Susan Morris, and several papers with the name Brian Morris.

Morris, that was something of a coincidence, Hilda's third gentleman had been a Mr Morris, Vernon Morris, she did hope he wasn't a relative of these people, although Morris was a fairly common name. She didn't really know much about her Mr Morris. The man had only been at Merrydown Crescent for about ten days when Hilda had given him a mickey finn in the form of valerian tablets. He had complained of a headache, and Hilda had offered him the tablets, telling him they were a herbal analgesic which would send him to sleep and cure his headache. She had omitted to mention that he wouldn't be waking up again.

He'd obediently swallowed the tablets, drunk his hot chocolate and drifted peaceably off to sleep. Hilda had strangled him with another home made garrotte. Her reason for getting rid of him so quickly was quite simple. She didn't want to get fond of him. She had quite enjoyed the company of Mr Smith, and had felt a genuine pang of remorse when he had died. Mr Bartlett had simply been a nuisance, always complaining, never satisfied. He had actually dared to criticise her cooking. In Hilda's opinion he wasn't worth keeping. Mr Smith had always eaten anything put in front of him. Mr Morris had all the makings of a quiet, compatible guest. It would be a wrench if she grew to like him and then had to do away with him. This way had been much better. He was gone, buried in the coal cellar next to Mr Bartlett. He hadn't suffered, and she had yet another bank account to plunder.

Hilda went back into the master bedroom. She had noticed a collection of photographs on the dressing tables. There were a couple of wedding photographs with them, and Hilda studied the faces of the families intently. There was no one amongst them with any resemblance to her Mr Morris. From what she could tell, this branch of the Morris family tended to run to sturdily built amongst their men folk. Hilda's penchant was for small, frail and slight in her paying guests, they were easier to dispose of.

She wandered back into the living room and flicked on the television. She would be in time for Weakest Link, she liked that. She would sit and shout the answers at the screen, she was in point of fact very clever with general knowledge questions, and she nearly always got them right. She would like to take part on the show, she was sure she could beat Ann Robinson at her own game when it came to trading insults, but she knew that she wouldn't be able to cope if she was voted off as a Weakest Link. And they would reject her at an early stage. She had seen it happen before, someone who was clever and intelligent and knew lots of general knowledge was soon voted off in tactical voting. All of the other contestants would quickly realise she was the best and get rid of her. She settled back, glancing at the clock. Five fifteen. Just in time. The TV screen flickered and the sports results came on. What? Of course, it was Saturday. Hilda had lost track of the days in her headlong flight.

She simply sat there for several minutes, staring blankly at the screen. Sport held no interest for her but she realised she was very tired, too languid to do much. Eventually boredom roused her into action. She jabbed at the remote control and changed channels just as the adverts came on. The first one was for an on-line fashion catalogue, the advertiser was exhorting customers to buy before 9pm tonight for delivery on the next working day. Hilda perked up and gazed intently at the web address, her lips working soundlessly as she repeated it to herself. She went through to the study, the computer was still on, in sleep mode. She pressed enter and it sprang into life. She quickly typed in the catalogue address and studied the screen intently. A plan was forming in her mind. She remembered the disdain in which the waitress at the tearooms had held her as she had sat at the table in her dowdy brown woollen coat. She needed to look the part she was playing, that of a well off mature woman, out and about on her travels.

Hilda let the cursor move over the pages of the catalogue. At first, out of habit, she looked for the cheapest articles. It took her several minutes to realise that she could choose anything she wanted, she wouldn't be paying for them herself. Hilda had a good eye for colour and style, and she soon chose several stunning outfits and dresses. She moved onto lingerie, she needed more than one change of underwear, and she could get herself a couple of those expensive girdles, give herself a bit of shape. Hilda was wise enough to know that her figure could best be described as dumpy. What else? A couple of pairs of shoes, some comfortable slippers and a decent sized handbag. Hilda usually liked to try shoes on when she bought them but she would just have to risk it this time. If they didn't fit, she would leave them behind for Susan Morris as a thank you for your hospitality gift.

She scrolled through the pages until she found a page dedicated to luggage. She chose a large wheeled suitcase in a cheerful red tartan, she did like tartan, and it had a matching overnight case. Everything would fit nicely in there. She carefully filled out the checkout details with Susan Morris's credit card details and hotmail address. Susan had left her account on "remember me" and "remember my password" so all Hilda had to do was open the emails, and get the confirmation that her order would arrive the next working day. That would be Monday morning, there would be no deliveries round here on a Sunday. Hilda wondered if Susan Morris was usually so lax with her computer security, or whether the excitement of a surprise holiday had knocked everything else out of the young woman's head?

Chapter 7

Barbara Grey parked her car in the car park of the Journey Lodge hotel, and contemplated the façade of the building. This was where the Hopkins woman had slept the night before last. Sunday was Barbara's rest day this week, but she knew she wouldn't be able to settle to anything at home. Barcroft was lucky, she thought, he had his wife and children to distract him, and he wasn't in DI Brent's bad books either. She allowed her mind to wander for a few moments. She really fancied her team partner Clive Barcroft, but he was a married man. Happily married too by the snippets of information he let slip. She had to be careful not to let her heart rule her head. No good would come of starting an affair, even if he felt the same way as she did which hardly seemed likely.

Barbara was ambitious, and the shock she had had on Friday when Hilda Hopkins had escaped had seriously rattled her. She had come within a hair's breadth of suspension. Consequently she was prepared to give up her own free time to see if she could track the woman down. It would feel so wonderful to apprehend her. This was personal now.

Barbara wondered which way Hilda Hopkins would have left the hotel. By all accounts she hadn't left by the lobby, she had disappeared while the police officers were in Reception. Barbara frowned resentfully, she bet they hadn't been reprimanded, just commiserated with for their bad luck. She was thankful it hadn't been her though, not a second time.

She locked her car and walked round the side of the building. There was a door along there, but when Barbara tried it, it was locked. It may have been open yesterday though, perhaps when the chambermaids were cleaning the rooms. Barbara walked across the car park, avoiding the front of the building. She scrambled over the low wall with considerably less grace than Hilda had shown, and looked up and down the street. If Hopkins had come this way, which way would she have turned? Well there were only two choices, left or right. She would follow both routes, work her way round from both directions.

Barbara strode purposefully down the road, looking about her keenly. She had no idea what she was looking for, she doubted that the woman would suddenly appear in front of her, she just wanted to try and see if she could retrace some of her steps. Barbara walked down the road, past a café and plunged into the small streets leading down to the canal. There weren't many people around, certainly there was no sign of her quarry. She came out on the tow path of the canal. They'd found Mr Johnson in the canal. He had floated up from the bottom of the lock much to the consternation of a passing jogger. It was that which had kick started the whole investigation once they had identified the man and discovered the address where he had been living. A plastic driving licence had slipped down through the torn lining of his pocket. Hilda had obviously missed that when she had dumped Mr Johnson's body in the water.

Hilda had been out when the police had first knocked at her front door, but the next door neighbour had said that there seemed to be a new man there nearly every week just lately. All elderly, all lodgers of "that Hopkins woman, interfering old cow that she is" as the neighbour had bitterly described her.

Well she was not likely to have swum down the canal reflected Barbara. She couldn't imagine the old biddy rowing herself away in a boat either, the woman was no spring chicken after all. A movement caught her eye, and she watched as a barge chugged slowly up the canal and spluttered to a standstill. Barbara walked briskly towards it, taking in the fact that canal barge trips took place from here. She waited while the crew went through their mooring manoeuvres, before approaching a young man who had just leapt onto the tow path. She flashed her warrant card and asked if she could have a word.

The man eyed her warily, and gave a perfunctory nod.

"I'm looking for an elderly lady who has gone walk about," explained Barbara, "I wondered if you'd seen anyone like that on your boat yesterday? Female, elderly, a bit plump, grey hair?"

"We get a lot like that, this time of year," replied the boatman, "it's a popular run from here to Neston. We did have some elderly folk on the boat yesterday, but I couldn't say if your old lady was definitely amongst them."

"Neston? Is that the first stop?"

"It's the only stop, we don't go any farther down the canal than Neston. Just there and back again, not the most exciting journey in the world but it's a good little earner during the summer months."

Barbara thanked him, and stood contemplating the water. It would make sense, Hilda Hopkins could have left Midchester on the boat easily enough. The police were watching the railway station and the bus station, but apparently no-one had considered the canal. She might be on to something. She needed to tread warily though, she didn't want to draw D I Brent's attention to her again too soon, especially if she was mistaken. She made up her mind, she would drive to Neston, and have a look around there. If nothing else, it would be a nice trip out into the countryside.

Hilda had finished her lunch, washed everything up and replaced it all where it came from. Apart from the inroads into the food, she was keen to leave no trace of her incursion. Hopefully the Morris's would either not notice the missing items, or would think that that Mrs O'Grady, the woman who cleaned for them was responsible. Hilda had no scruples about ruining another woman's honest reputation.

She returned to the small study. She had the glimmerings of an idea for moving on from here. The owners would be back by the end of the week, she mustn't get too comfortable. Tomorrow her new clothes would arrive, so maybe by Wednesday, or Thursday at the latest she should be on her way elsewhere.

Hilda looked up coach trips for the over fifties. She came across one company who advertised tailor made trips. They were quite expensive. Their speciality was to collect their customers from home and ferry them to a central meeting point to join the coach before setting off to various venues. Hilda checked the timetable and discovered there was a coach this coming Tuesday. It was a circular tour, taking in several famous gardens and Houses and included a two day visit to Danemouth, a pretty coastal resort. Hilda quite liked gardens, she had worked hard at Merrydown Crescent in order to make sure her front garden was always in immaculate order. The back garden had been something of a wilderness, but that had been all the better when she needed somewhere to bury her paying guests. A grave in the middle of her front lawn would surely have excited comment, even from her dull neighbours.

And this trip included a visit to the seaside, that would be wonderful. It had been years since Hilda had had a seaside holiday. She carefully gathered all the stuff she thought she would need, credit card, hotmail address, the postcode for this bungalow, and reached for the phone. She dialled the customer services number shown on the screen, and enquired about trips to Danemouth.

"Actually we do have one cancellation for this Tuesday," said the helpful voice on the other end of the phone, "you are lucky, madam, someone dropped out at the last minute. It's not a direct journey to Danemouth, more of a circular tour with Danemouth included, and it's not a window seat I'm afraid, but if you are interested........?"

Hilda was very interested. She booked the seat in the name of Susan Morris, paid the amount asked, on Susan's credit card, and gave the address for the taxi pick up.

"It'll be a very early start, Mrs Morris," explained the caller, "the taxi will call for you at six thirty on Tuesday morning. Will you be able to manage that?"

Hilda assured her that she would be up and ready in plenty of time........

Chapter 8

Barbara Grey had never visited Neston before. It wasn't really on the way to anywhere, and it was out of her own patrol area. She found a parking space easily enough, near the passage which led down to the canal. The place looked very sleepy. Barbara strolled down the main street. There were two tearooms, "The Singing Canary" and "The Willow Tree Tea Room". Both were closed. Barbara checked the opening times. The Singing Canary would be open from 2pm, but the Willow Tree was closed all day on Sundays. Would it be worth while waiting until 2pm she wondered? What would she do round here for the better part of two hours?

She walked on down the road. There was a hall, with a ripped poster on the outside wall announcing that there had been a jumble sale there on the previous day. Several black bags were piled neatly to one side of the door. Unsaleable jumble waiting to go to the dump she supposed.

There was a flurry of movement ahead of her. Barbara hurried across the street. People were streaming out of the church, evidently it was the end of the morning service. The vicar stood in the doorway of the church, shaking hands with his parishioners. Three choir boys, still in their surplices were chasing around the gravestones.

"How very English," the thought popped unbidden into Barbara's mind.

The vicar broke the spell by shouting at the boys to go back inside the church. Barbara gave herself a mental shake. She wasn't here sightseeing. All the time she was scanning the faces of the women as they passed through the lych-gate, although she doubted if Hilda Hopkins would have the gall to enter a church considering what she had been up to.

There was no sign of her. Barbara returned to her car and drove around the village. It didn't take long, it was a very small village. There appeared to be no hotel here, but the local Inn advertised rooms to let on a board next to the door of the Public Bar. Barbara went in and flashed her warrant card at the landlord. This wasn't really her jurisdiction, but it would be such a feather in her cap if she tracked the miserable woman down.

There was no-one staying there though, no-one at all, and they hadn't had any guests for some time. The landlord explained that although they had the board up advertising rooms, they didn't actively seek guests, he felt they were often more trouble than they were worth. There was a nice B & B in the village, Wisteria Lodge, he normally tried to steer any would be guests in that direction.

Barbara took the address of Wisteria Lodge and followed the directions the landlord had given her. The Lodge turned out to be a large chalet bungalow in a road of smaller bungalows. Barbara rang the doorbell and was shown into a neat sitting room by a middle aged man who gave his name as Mr Hartley. Barbara flashed her warrant card, and explained that she was concerned about the whereabouts of an elderly lady who had gone missing. Without actually saying so, Barbara gave the impression that the old lady suffered from memory loss, Alzheimer's and dementia hung unspoken in the air between them.

"Can't help you, I'm afraid m'dear," replied Hartley, regretfully, "we've got a Mr and Mrs Broome staying here at the moment. They are from the States and are over here looking for their roots. Well Mrs Broome's roots actually. Mrs Broome's ancestors were from around here apparently. The other room is vacant just now. Would you care to see it?"

He was obviously proud of his home, and Barbara accepted the invitation to look round. The single bedroom was made up, ready for its next guest, a pretty room looking out over a garden overshadowed by high hedges. The double bedroom next door showed signs of occupancy by two people. Hilda could not have acquired a partner and an American accent in the space of two days. Asked, Mr Hartley said that the couple had been staying here since Wednesday last, so that was that.

Barbara thanked the man for his hospitality and returned to her car. Maybe Hopkins hadn't travelled to Neston on the barge, or if she had, she had continued her journey elsewhere under her own steam in some way. This definitely seemed to be a dead end, unless, she thought with a grim smile, the wretched woman had slept amongst the tombstones last night. Barbara accelerated down the street, passing the bungalow, three doors away from Wisteria Lodge, where Hilda Hopkins was settled on the Morris's sofa, a plate of biscuits to hand, watching one of her favourite films on the television.

Chapter 9

Hilda was up bright and early on Tuesday morning. She had spent the previous day making sure that she had left no obvious signs of her stay. The credit card had been returned to its place, and the history on the computer had been cleared. All the emails to Susan regarding the clothing and other purchases, plus the information about her planned coach trip had been deleted. Hilda had stripped the bed and washed the sheets before stuffing them into the tumble dryer. She slept on the bare mattress that night, and remade the bed in the morning. The sitting room had been hoovered, the curtains opened, while all the crockery she had used was washed and stacked neatly in the wall unit where she had found it. The cutlery too had been cleaned and replaced in its drawer. She even managed to plug the microwave oven back in, although she shuddered as she did so. Hilda had a genuine though irrational fear of microwaves.

Hilda had packed her old clothes along with the new. It had crossed her mind they might be useful at some point as a disguise. She looked at the shopping trolley she had bought at the jumble sale. She wouldn't be able to take that as well, she only had one pair of hands. Regretfully Hilda took the thing to bits and stuffed all the pieces into a black bag, together with the odd remainders of food that she had purloined. With a bit of luck, the Morris's wouldn't realise that anything was missing from their kitchen. The black bag went out with the bins, it would be long gone before the Morris's returned at the end of the week. As to the purchases on the credit card, hopefully if the woman received a monthly statement, it would be another three weeks before she noticed the extra spending on there.

Hilda Hopkins was neatly dressed in a powder blue suit whose colour suited her perfectly. The girdle had made all the difference to the fit, and she looked quite elegant in her smart new shoes and matching handbag.

Hilda lurked by the front door, listening for the taxi. As soon as she heard it draw up at the front gate, she let herself out, slipped the key back under the flowerpot and met the driver halfway down the path. He took her luggage from her, and opened the door so that she could settle herself in the back seat. Hilda smiled grimly to herself. What a difference the hint of money, and nice clothes made to people's attitudes.

She settled back in the seat as the taxi set off. A holiday, a real little holiday, just what she needed after all the stress and excitement she'd experienced lately. She dipped her head and gazed at her lap as two police cars swept past on the other side of the road, heading into Neston.

"Unusual to see two of them around here," muttered the driver, glancing into his driving mirror, "wonder where they are off to?"

"They are like buses," replied Hilda brightly, "you wait ages for one, then two come along together."

The driver laughed appreciatively as he changed gears before tackling the steep hill which took them out of Neston.

Chapter 10

Barbara Grey picked up her breakfast tray and looked around the crowded police canteen. Over in the far corner Detective Constable Graham Perkins sat alone at a table. Barbara wended her way across to him.

"Can I join you? This place is choc a block today."

Perkins glanced up and nodded.

"Feel free Barbara. Clive not with you?"

"He'll be along in a few minutes, he's just sorting something out."

Perkins looked at Barbara, with her clear skin and softly waved auburn hair she would make an ideal model for a police recruitment poster he thought.

Barbara stirred her coffee wondering how she would bring up the subject of Hilda Hopkins and her own thoughts about Neston.

"So," Perkins groped for something to say, "how was your weekend? Do anything interesting."

It was the perfect opening.

"I had a potter around Midchester, down by the canal. They have barge trips from there, they cruise up to Neston and back. I thought I'd mention it to Clive."

"Oh yes," grinned Perkins.

Barbara scowled at him.

"So that he can take Lillian and the kids for a day out. He is a married man, Graham. Children love boats, and that would be something a bit different. It's not expensive either."

Perkins coloured and mumbled something incoherent.

Clive Barcroft arrived at the table.

"Room for a little one? Hi Graham, how's it going?"

He sat down and the two men started a conversation about United's performance the previous Saturday. Barbara ate her bacon sandwich, wondering if the seed she had planted in Perkins' mind would grow into something definite. Would he pass on the tip about the canal trips to Claire Naylor, or even Detective Inspector Brent?

Chapter 11

The taxi had stopped by a long coach drawn up outside The Royal Oak on the outskirts of Midchester, and the driver informed Hilda that they had arrived at the departure point. He carried her luggage across to the coach for her and saw it safely stowed away in the hold. Hilda wasn't sure whether she was supposed to tip the driver or not. The trip was expensive and he presumably got paid for each trip he did, so she decided she wouldn't bother. Hilda still had her sense of frugality despite the roll of notes secreted in her new handbag.

The courier swooped down to greet her.

"Hello there, my name is Hazel, and I'm here to make your journey as comfortable as possible. Anything you need, you must just ask."

She was dressed in a bottle green and gold suit that matched the livery of the coach. Hilda thought it very tasteful, if a little old fashioned looking.

"I don't have a ticket," said Hilda, "I was told to quote 10372?"

"Oh yes, Mrs Morris, you are our last minute replacement." Hazel gave a tinkling laugh. "I'll show you your seat; you'll be sitting with Miss Leverson."

Hilda didn't much care who she would be sitting with so long as she was on the coach and away from the road. Despite her little joke, she was a little unsettled by the two police cars which she had seen heading into Neston.

Hazel bustled along the aisle of the coach, prattling away, and Hilda followed her. Her seat she found was about halfway down the coach, and she saw a small mousey woman already ensconced in the window seat, reading through a brochure.

"Here's our new passenger," said Hazel gaily, "I'm sure you two will get on famously."

Her smile faltered slightly at the expression on Hilda's face. Hilda realised she had to keep up the pretence of a well to do, and presumably well mannered lady. She stiffly moved her features into the semblance of a smile, confessed to being tired, not used to such an early start, and agreed that the coming excursion sounded very exciting.

Hazel retreated towards the front of the coach in search of more new passengers and Hilda settled herself in her seat. Her neighbour was still engrossed in the brochure. Hilda gazed past her into the street.

Another taxi had arrived. A woman with a blue rinse that was nearly purple disembarked, calling out to someone still in the back seat. The taxi rocked slightly as the occupant moved across the seat and backed out before standing up and looking around him.

Hilda gave an audible gasp and clutched at her breast. The man was the image of Mr Tompkins. But he was safely buried in the earth behind her shed in Merrydown Crescent...... well probably not now, the police wouldn't have left him there, he'd be in the mortuary by now. Hilda leaned forward slightly. No, this man was taller than Mr Tompkins, but the similarity was marked. Mr Tompkins had had a small moustache, much like that worn by David Niven, a toothbrush moustache, but this man was clean shaven.

Hilda strained her ears to catch the name of the couple. Hazel was escorting them down the coach to a seat a few rows behind Hilda.

"You are by the window, Mrs Toddington-Smythe, Mr Toddington-Smythe you have the aisle seat."

Toddington-Smythe, so not Tompkins, but just take the moustache off Mr Tompkins' effigy, and it would do for this man too! Hilda had had something of a fright, she gave herself a little shake and giggled quietly to herself. Miss Leverson in the next seat looked at her in alarm.

"Sorry, just thinking about something funny," murmured Hilda, "private joke."

She'd had a bit of trouble with that moustache of Mr Tompkins'. She'd tried embroidering it onto his face at first, but it came out too bushy. She carefully snipped the pieces of thread away and tried again, using smaller stitches. This time she was left with an aging Adolf Hitler. The small square moustache and the lick of hair falling across the forehead had given the man an uncanny resemblance to the late German Dictator. In the end she had used a fine permanent marker just to hint at the facial hair.

In character Mr Tompkins couldn't have been farther away from the despot though. He had been a very quietly spoken man, calm and unruffled, no histrionics. Not that Hilda had known him for very long. This one had only lasted five days, he had hardly had chance to get his feet under the table. It had been his own fault of course ruminated Hilda. She had found him in the back garden, poking around the back of the shed. Mr Abbott was already there, about three foot under the ground, and Hilda's heart had thumped uncomfortably in her chest as Mr Tompkins surveyed the area of dug earth.

She had made up a tale that she wanted to have a patio out here, perhaps change the shed for a summerhouse, and have barbecues during the long summer evenings. Mr Tompkins had nodded thoughtfully, before stirring the ground with his toe.

Hilda had shivered slightly, and commented that there was a chill in air this evening; Mr Tompkins should really come indoors, he would catch his death out here. Obediently Mr Tompkins had turned and followed Hilda into the kitchen. And that was where he had caught his death before accompanying Mr Abbott behind the garden shed. Hilda settled back comfortably as the excursion began.

The coach swept into the car park of King's Abbott Manor House and the passengers were disgorged. Hazel, the cheerful courier, swiftly divided her charges into two groups, those who were going to do the House, and those who wanted to roam around the gardens. Hilda joined the latter group, alongside her travelling companion, Miss Leverson. Each group moved off, and Hilda quickly left the others to wander off by herself. She came across a bench overlooking the rose garden, with the mellow pile of the Manor House just beyond, and sat down to enjoy the view.

King's Abbott. Her Mr Abbott had been quite kingly, she thought, he had had a regal air about him. It was the way he held himself, despite his advanced years he had something of a military bearing, straight backed, brisk in manner. Although a short man, below average height, he appeared taller, there had been a presence about him. He had kept himself beautifully turned out too. Hilda had scented money when she first interviewed him. Once he had moved in, he set up an ironing board in his bedroom, and spent a lot of his time pressing his shirts and trousers so that they were impeccable. Hilda kept a clean and tidy house, but ironing was something she abhorred. She very rarely bothered, choosing clothes that were fairly crease resistant and could simply be washed and dried and worn again.

Hilda had planned in advanced for the disposal of Mr Abbott. The coal hole was full up now that she had Mr Bartlett and Mr Morris packed in there.

She didn't want to risk taking another body along the tow path. She had been lucky with Mr Smith, but the risks were really too great. Behind the shed in the corner of Hilda's garden there was a depression in the ground. This was left over from the Second World War and had been the site of the old Anderson shelter now long gone, but there was still something of a hole left. Hilda took her spade and began to dig. It was hard going, but she eventually had a small trench dug.

She didn't encourage her gentlemen to use the garden, and she was taken by surprise when Mr Abbott appeared around the side of the shed and asked her what she was doing. Hilda started, and leaned on her spade, a little breathless.

"I want to pave this bit over," she replied brightly, "make a patio out of it. Perhaps replace the shed with a proper summer house. I thought it would be nice to have a barbecue down here in the summer, away from the houses so that the smoke doesn't waft over."

Hilda had had several acrimonious arguments with her neighbours over the years when smoke from their barbecues had drifted into her sitting room.

"You should get a man in to do that for you," commented Mr Abbott gravely, "you'll do yourself damage Mrs Hopkins, slaving like that at your age."

She'd bridled at the reference to her age, but managed a lop sided though gracious smile as Mr Abbott had reached for the spade, offering to dig over the patch a bit more for her. He'd made a good job of it too, she reflected, despite his own advanced years.

She'd killed him that night. He was already tired from his efforts, and the valerian tablets in his coffee had finished the job, sending him into a deep sleep in his chair. Hilda already had the new garrotte ready and despatched the old man quickly and neatly. It took quite a while to bury him, and she had earth left over when she finished,. She scattered that around the garden rather than leaving it humped over the grave. The ground was still uneven, but it didn't look like an obvious burial site once she had flattened the soil somewhat.

"Isn't it lovely," twittered a voice, "may I sit with you?"

Hilda looked up. It was Miss Leverson, her fellow passenger from the coach. Hilda put her handbag onto her lap and moved her ample hips along the bench, leaving room for the younger woman to sit down. Ideally she would have liked to have told her to go away, but Hilda was aware she mustn't draw any unwonted attention to herself.

They sat there in silence for several minutes, each drinking in the tranquil scene.

"Mother would have liked this," murmured Miss Leverson, "she would have loved poking around in the House."

'Great', thought Hilda, 'I'm saddled with one of the recently bereaved. I do hope she doesn't start weeping and wailing on the coach.'

She decided she had better show some sympathy to the blasted woman.

"I'm so sorry dear, did you lose your mother recently?"

"Oh Mother's not dead!" Miss Leverson looked slightly shocked, "she's eighty-six and determined to get her telegram from the Queen."

"Ahh right, sorry," muttered Hilda, "you didn't think of bringing her with you when your friend dropped out then?"

"Mary was rushed into hospital with appendicitis last week," explained Miss Leverson, "I dare say Mother would have liked to come, but the lady from Social Services said I had to have a break from caring. They've arranged for Mother to stay in a nice nursing home while I'm away."

For a moment she looked wistful.

"And then she'll come back once I'm home. I daresay she'll be a bit awkward for a while afterwards, she doesn't like change much, but I intend enjoying this holiday. I just wish Mary's appendix had held out a bit longer."

Hilda's mind had been working. The police were looking for a lone elderly woman. She could use this woman as camouflage. The police wouldn't take that much notice of a pair of women pottering about the place. How to reel her in though. Hilda had had very few friends during her life, and wasn't sure how to attract them. Perhaps the sympathy card?

"I'm on my own too," confided Hilda, "I er lost my husband years and years ago, and we weren't blessed with children." She paused before adding "maybe we could go round the House together?"

"That would be lovely," beamed Miss Leverson, "What shall I call you, my name's Lettice."

"Lettuce? I've not heard of that as a name before, is it a nick name?"

"Lettice with an "I"" replied Miss Leverson ruefully, "the girls at school used to call me Lettuce Leaf. Mary calls me Lettie. I know you are Mrs Morris, what's your first name?"

"Hil....." began Hilda, hastily amending it to "Hilary. I used to be called Hilly when I was younger."

She had a sudden vision of her five year old self being swung up in the strong arms of her father. He had been a giant bear of a man.

"Up, up and away, little Hilly, and over the mountain." He would dangle her over his shoulders as he said this, her nose pressed against his back, secure in the knowledge that she wouldn't be dropped.

She'd gone to school as usual one day, and a strange lady had come in at lunch time to take her to stay at the local children's home for a few days. When Hilda had returned home, her mother had told her that Daddy had gone to live with the angels, and that had been that. She'd learned years later that he had had a sudden fatal heart attack.

"I'll call you Hilly then," replied Lettie, who was bending down fiddling with the strap on her sandals and missed the expression on Hilda's face. "These are new and they are rubbing my foot a bit."

"Pour some hot water through them when we get to the hotel tonight, that'll soften them."

Hilda stood up and started to make her way towards the House with Lettie trailing in her wake.

Chapter 12

There was a choice of activities the next morning. Either a visit to the mediaeval church, or a chance to spend some time pottering around the shops. Hilda didn't want to go to the church, shopping held much more appeal for her. Lettie was undecided, and was prattling away trying to balance the pros and cons of a historic walk against the pleasures of shopping.

Hilda ignored her, she was too busy reading the newspaper. Her little gentlemen had made the nationals. There weren't any photographs of the dolls, but there was a picture of her house under the caption "Boarding House of Horrors." Boarding house, where had they got that from? It was a normal house with paying guests, one gentleman at a time too, it wasn't a bed and breakfast hotel, just bed and burial, Hilda giggled at her little joke. Lettie looked across the breakfast table and asked Hilly what was she reading?

"Just bits and pieces in the paper," replied Hilda. Lettie craned her neck to see the page.

"Oooh, I saw that on the news, isn't it dreadful? That woman must be a real monster. I'm so glad we're not going anywhere near that place, Hilly, Mother wouldn't like it if she thought I was exposed to that sort of thing."

Hilda frowned. "Mother wouldn't like it" was a frequent remark from Lettie. During the journey Lettie had confided to Hilda that she had never married because Mother hadn't considered that any of Lettie's young men were "suitable". Besides, Mother had said, an only daughter's place was at her mother's side, looking after her needs, time enough for dalliances once Mother was gone. Hilda had been amazed that anyone should think like that in this day and age. Hilda had always gone her own way, done what she wanted to do and blow anyone else's needs. It wasn't often that Hilda considered the idiosyncrasies of others, other than to work out how to use them for her own purposes, but she suspected that poor mousey Lettie had spent her life trying to please Mama, and the sad thing was, she would never succeed.

"Well it's certainly not the sort of thing I would expect to happen in Neston," replied Hilda, remembering that she was supposed to come from there, "ours is a respectable neighbourhood."

Chapter 13

The respectable neighbourhood was undergoing door by door enquiries by the police. Barbara Grey's seemingly casual comment to Detective Constable Perkins had borne fruit. Perkins had indeed passed on the information about the canal trips to Claire Naylor and John Brent, once told, had ordered the search area to be widened. Claire had shown Hilda's photograph, now enhanced with grey rather than brown hair, to the waitress in "The Willow Tree Tea Rooms". The girl, Bryony Fraser had havered for several minutes, saying she really couldn't say, she really wasn't sure, but there had been a woman in there on Saturday...... not quite their usual clientele, she had been wearing a coat which smelt faintly of mothballs, a brown woollen coat, completely unsuitable for the time of year, and a woolly hat. Claire had felt quietly triumphant. This matched the description that they had obtained from the Reception staff at the Journey Lodge.

"She looked like a bag lady. She had this awful shopping trolley. A sort of blue pattern I think, stuffed with all sorts of rubbish by the look of it. She left me 10p for a tip, I'd have thought better of her if she'd left nothing. 10p," the girl sniffed, "it's an insult. What do you want her for anyway?"

"We are pursuing enquiries," said Claire vaguely, "and we think she can help. Did you see where she went when she left here?"

"Sorry, I was just thankful to have her out of here. She had a sort of, I dunno, a sort of presence that was a bit malevolent. That sounds a bit melodramatic I know," she smiled, "I just wasn't comfortable somehow, I couldn't put my finger on it, just a feeling, you know? A sort of charisma in reverse."

Claire nodded, "woman's intuition. That's a useful instinct you have there, Bryony, hang on to it."

Chapter 14

Hilda had persuaded Lettie to forego the church visit and come shopping with her. Not that she particularly wanted Lettie's company, but once again she considered that two women out shopping would attract less interest than a lone shopper. The police, so far as she knew, were still looking for a solitary pensioner.

They were in a large newsagents shop. Lettie was trying to choose a suitable postcard to send to Mother. Apparently the old woman would expect a postcard every day. Hilda had spotted a machine knitting magazine. Should she buy it? Would the police have put out an order for any purchases of machine knitting books to be reported to them? They knew of her hobby after all. Hilda desperately wanted to buy the magazine, but would it be her undoing? She decided to compromise. She glanced around, no-one was looking. She stood and scanned through the pages. Looking at the photographs of the garments, which ones would she like to make, this cardigan perhaps, and that sweater was lovely with the cable detail round the neck.

A full page advertisement caught her eye. "Machine Knitting Exhibition" 10 am to 4pm, to be held at Danemouth Girls' High School." It was this Saturday, the day after tomorrow, and she would be there, in Danemouth. Hilda had attended an Exhibition years ago, in Bristol. It had been a wonderful day out. She hadn't been since, it was too far, but she would go to the Danemouth one this year. This would be her special treat. Hilda slipped the magazine back onto the rack, picked up a gossipy woman's magazine and went across to the till.

The excursion arrived in Danemouth just in time for dinner at their hotel. The porters came out and took charge of the luggage while Hazel sorted out the rooms. Hilda found herself allocated to a small single room at the back of the hotel, overlooking one of the long chines leading down to the beach. By rights she should have been sharing a twin room with Lettie as she had taken over her friend Mary's ticket, but Hazel had managed to get her a room on her own in each hotel they had stayed in so far. Hilda was pleased, she didn't want to share with a stranger, and what would happen if she talked in her sleep? Whether she did this or not she didn't know, but it wasn't safe to take the chance. She could have done away with Lettie if she had had any suspicions of course, another death at her door wouldn't faze her, but it would draw attention to the coach trip, and Hilda really wanted to keep a low profile.

Hilda glanced at the woman dozing in the seat next to her. Lettie really was a very trusting woman. Hilda could easily slip into her room any night and just smother her in her sleep. It had been a couple of weeks now since Hilda had last killed. She loved the thrill that went through her when she felt the spirit leaving the men's bodies. The knowledge that she, Hilda Hopkins, had absolute power over life or death was intoxicating. Lettie's head lolled against Hilda's shoulder and she snored gently. Hilda sat rigidly, hating the feel of another human being in such close proximity to her. Would she risk another killing? Hilda gradually relaxed, probably not; Lettie had been very useful to her in her own innocent and unwitting way. Besides, thought Hilda, with a grim smile, it wouldn't really do for Lettice Leverson to end up as a murder victim, Mother wouldn't like it!

After dinner most of the party retired to the Lounge to watch the television. There was a small segment about the Merrydown Crescent murders. Police enquiries had been extended out to Neston, where there had been a positive sighting of Hilda Hopkins. The Morris's were due back about now. Would they have noticed that anything was amiss in their home?

Hilda needed to make plans. She really wanted to visit the Knitting Machine Exhibition. She would probably be safe for that, they wouldn't have worked out yet where she was. She was far cleverer than they were, she knew that. So, tomorrow she would go to the Exhibition. She would tell Hazel she had been called back home. Some sort of domestic crisis, that would do. She would go along to the railway station and take the first train out to wherever. It would be exciting seeing where she would end up.

She went back up to her room and checked the money in her handbag. There was quite a considerable amount. Hilda sat and cogitated. Eventually she came to a decision. She sorted the money into four lots. Three lots went into plastic bags, the fourth share was returned to her handbag. She slipped downstairs and walked out, heading towards the shopping centre. She bought a child's spade from a souvenir shop and made her way towards the fringes of the town. There were long valleys, called chines, leading down towards the sea.

Hilda dug holes in the side of the chine, and buried each bag of money. She was careful to note landmarks, a gorse bush here, an outcrop of rock there. Once all the money was safely stashed away, she climbed higher up the chine, dug a hole, laid the spade in it, wrapped in a carrier bag, and smoothed the ground back over it. She might not have a spade if she needed to come back and dig up the money, a bit of forethought, that was what was needed. That was what made her a cut above ordinary killers, she was much better at the planning aspect of it all.

Chapter 15

"Sarge, Sarge," Barbara Grey hurried into the incident room, waving a brightly coloured magazine, "look at this."

She laid the magazine in front of Claire Naylor. Naylor picked it up.

"It's a knitting mag, so what?" she asked.

"The Hopkins woman. She's into that machine knitting malarkey, look at this," she repeated, opening the magazine at a page with a turned down corner, "there's a convention or Exhibition or something. And it's taking place tomorrow in Danemouth. Anyway, it's a big day out for machine knitters. I bet we'll find her there."

Claire sat back and perused the advertisement.

"She's on the run for multiple murders, is she likely to pop off for a day's knitting?" she asked.

"She's certainly full of herself enough to," replied Barbara, "have there been any other sightings of her Sarge, since Neston?"

"Nothing," admitted Claire, "but how would she have got to Danemouth. It's nearly fifty miles from here?"

"Flew on her broomstick like the old witch she is," suggested Barbara venomously. "I have no idea Sarge, but much as I dislike the woman, I think she would be capable of getting there somehow. You've seen her workroom, she's obviously besotted with the subject. She even made trophies of her victims in knitting. I just feel it's somewhere she would gravitate to."

Claire ran her hand through her short hair and looked at the magazine.

"It's not our jurisdiction, we'll have to get the Danemouth police to stake the place out," decided Claire, "I'll have a word with the boss."

"That won't work," retorted Barbara, "look at the picture." The advertisement showed a crowd of visitors from the previous year's exhibition. The majority of the women ranged from middle aged to elderly, and many of the women had white hair. "She'd disappear amongst that lot, they'd never spot her. Can't we go, we know her."

"Let me speak to the boss," repeated Claire. "We'd have to liaise with the Danemouth lot whichever way we do it. Can't go round stepping on other Forces' toes Barbara."

She looked at the younger woman's anxious face and suggested she went and changed into her uniform for her shift while she spoke to John Brent. Reluctantly Barbara acquiesced. She would have to find Clive Barcroft and tell him all about her idea. They were on lates today so he should be here at any minute.

Claire hadn't returned when it was time for Grey and Barcroft to go out on patrol. Barbara was on tenterhooks. She really felt that they were on to something. She let Barcroft drive, she felt too keyed up to concentrate on driving.

"She needs to be caught Clive. She has to spend the rest of her life in prison, she's just too dangerous to be left out in the community. Surely she must be tired of being on the run, she must know we'll catch up with eventually. I'm just afraid she'll kill again if she gets cornered somewhere. The woman has no conscience."

"Just relax, Barb, I'm sure the Sarge will chat Brent into following up your lead."

"Maybe," replied Barbara, "I just want to be in at the kill!"

Chapter 16

When Hilda walked into the Danemouth Machine Knitting Exhibition, she felt that she had come home. All around her were stalls selling patterns, yarns and all the minutiae of machine knitting. A Fashion Show was advertised for half past one, and there were a couple of workshops later in the afternoon which Hilda decided she would like to attend. She had several hundred pounds in her handbag, the rest of the money was safely stashed away in one of the long chines that dotted the coast around here. A useful little back up if she needed to go on the run again. Hilda was proving to be a quick learner.

She had thought she would have a problem with Lettie. For the past three days the two women had been almost joined at the hip. Hilda found her new companion a little wearing. She was used to doing what she wanted, when she wanted, and she had found cooperating with another person very difficult indeed. Thankfully Lettie had wanted to go on the optional excursion to the Aquarium. Hilda had said that she had no interest in fish, other than on a plate with a mound of chips, well doused in salt and vinegar, and declared her intention of walking around some of the antique shops in Danemouth. She had dutifully waved Lettie off after breakfast and set out to find the venue of the Machine Knitting Exhibition with Lettie's wishes for her to have a good time still ringing in her ears..

Hilda knew she would have to try and find a permanent place to stay so that she could get a new knitting machine. Well a second hand machine of course, but it would be new to her. She really missed her knitting. She could take up hand knitting again in the meantime, but she loved the possibilities that a machine opened up to her. Even if she was just staying in a bed sit she would find room to set one up. It could live in a corner of the room. Her mind buzzed with possibilities.

She strolled around, looking at all the exhibits, handling the fabrics, running her fingers down the cones of yarn to test their softness. She paused by the Knit and Knatter stall where the knitters were sitting working on Dorset buttons. She watched fascinated as one woman picked up a small plastic curtain ring, then deftly covered the edges with blanket stitch. Several spokes of yarn were stretched over the ring before the woman began to weave the yarn in and out, her needle flashing under the light, as she filled in the centre.

'What an excellent idea' thought Hilda. She could make those to match her jackets, instead of searching high and low for buttons of the same colour as the yarn. And what else? Yes, draughts, or checkers as the Americans called the game. If she made twelve white buttons and twelve black ones and knitted a board in black and white squares she could make a travelling draughts game. Hilda liked playing draughts. She had occasionally played the game with some of her gentlemen, those who had managed to stay with her for some weeks of course.

She started to go through the calculations, seven stitches and ten rows to a square inch. She would need a board eight squares long by eight squares wide. One inch wide squares might be a little too small, maybe two inches. That would be one hundred and sixty rows long and fourteen by eight stitches wide. She stood there, engrossed in mental arithmetic. Four eights were thirty-two, add eighty that would be, yes, one hundred and twelve stitches. She would only need to punch out two rows on the punch card, she could lock the card so long as she was careful about changing the colours every twenty rows. If she backed the squares, she could make a pocket to keep the playing pieces in, maybe sew a zip across the top so that the pieces were all kept tidily in place. Hilda was nearly dizzy with delight; her mind was brimming over with ideas.

At the front door, Detective Sergeant Claire Naylor, accompanied by PC Barbara Grey, was speaking earnestly to the Exhibition Organiser. Both women showed their warrant cards, and were ushered through into the main hall. Two officers from the local Force stayed on guard by the front entrance.

Hilda had wandered away from the Knit and Knatter stall. She headed towards a small room just off the Main Hall. One of the helpers was beavering away at a tuck stitch lace scarf on a machine similar to the one which Hilda had used. She looked up at Hilda and smiled.

"Would you like to have a go?" she asked cheerfully.

Hilda changed places with her with alacrity. She looked at the punch card, and the set up of the needles, looking to see which needles were out of work to form the "holes" of the lace, and which were set to tuck the yarn to give a delicate ruffled appearance. She lovingly took hold of the carriage handle, and in a single smooth, fluid movement pushed the carriage across the needle bed. It felt so good. Hilda swung into the familiar rhythm, passing the carriage back and forth, not too far, but making sure she cleared the edge of the stitches. The scarf grew in length in front of her eyes. She must make a note of the needle set up and the number of the punchcard that was being used, this was a lovely pattern, it would be a useful addition to her library.

A hand gripped Hilda's shoulder as Detective Sergeant Claire Naylor recited the Police Caution………….

"Hilda Beatrice Hopkins, I am arresting you on suspicion of the murder of Albert Johnson and there may be other charges to follow…… You do not have to say anything, but it may harm your defence if you do not mention when questioned something which you later rely on in court, anything you do say may be given in evidence."

Hilda's hand shot out and grasped a large ribber weight sitting on the table behind the knitting machine. Like a flash she snatched it up and dropped it onto Claire Naylor's foot.

The Detective Sergeant let out a squawk of anguish and hopped back, bending down to try and clutch at her injured foot. Hilda sprang out of her chair and sprinted towards the door with a surprising turn of speed for someone of her age and stature.

PC Barbara Grey stepped into the doorway and seized hold of Hilda's arm, snapping a pair of handcuffs onto one wrist, before twisting the woman's other arm to complete the action, pinioning her arms effectively behind her. Claire Naylor had taken the seat which Hilda had so rapidly vacated. Grey grinned over Hilda's shoulder,

"You okay Sarge?"

"I think my big toe is broken," replied Naylor through gritted teeth. "Give Barcroft a call on your radio, Barbara, get him in here to give us a hand. You can drop me at Casualty on the way to the Station."

Flanked by Constables Barcroft and Grey, Hilda Hopkins was escorted out to the waiting police car. A crowd of people had abandoned the Exhibition to come out and gawp as the trio made their way across the car park, with Detective Sergeant Naylor limping in the rear.

As the back door of the car was opened, Hilda looked round haughtily at the onlookers. A line from one of her favourite Fu Manchu films came into her mind. She drew herself up to her full five foot four inches and announced in stentorian tones....

"The world shall hear of me again."

Hilda Hopkins, Bed and Burial

Vivienne Fagan

Chapter 1

The windswept cliff top looked innocent enough thought Hilda Hopkins. She was sitting by her bedroom window gazing through a gap in the pine trees. No-one would guess the grim secret it held.

She could hear the surf pounding on the beach beneath the cliffs. They had had quite a good summer, herself and Abigail Moffat, there was a tidy sum in the bank, although Hilda had her own plans as to the redistribution of that. There were also six bodies secreted at the back of the cave which Hilda had found in the side of the cliff. She calculated they might be able to park another seven bodies in there before they ran out of space. Well maybe half a dozen, six plus seven was thirteen, an unlucky number.

It was the low season now for the holiday trade, and this Guest House, the Travellers' Rest, was not a particularly popular venue for holiday makers even at the height of the season. It was too far out of the village, too close to the top of the cliff, and it still had a gloomy old fashioned air about it despite a new lick of paint and the tiny garden to the front. Still, there were the special clientele who occasionally found their way to this out of the way spot. Apart from the pine trees, nothing much grew along here. The wind whistled along the top of the cliffs discouraging any new green shoots that dared to poke through the unfriendly earth.

Hilda had arrived at Travellers' Rest two years previously. She had been trying to get to Danemouth, but had ended up at the small out of the way coastal resort of Grime's Cove instead. There had been too much police activity around Danemouth itself, and Hilda had a special reason for not coming within their sphere. She was a convicted serial killer, having made away with five men, all paying guests in her home. Not all at once of course, she had topped them one by one, only getting caught when, having run out of places to bury her gentlemen, one of them had floated up from the bottom of the canal lock. Hilda had escaped and had been on the run for over a week, living on her wits, before the police had caught up with her at the Danemouth Machine Knitting Exhibition.

Hilda was an ardent machine knitter. She had despatched her gentlemen using garrotes which she had knitted herself, and as a memorial, she had knitted a small doll for each of her victims. Beautifully crafted, startlingly lifelike, they had adorned her house until the day the police had appeared at the door.

Hilda had stormed through the Magistrates Court and the Crown Court like an avenging spirit. She had made no protestations of innocence. Indeed, she was proud of her achievements. Staying on remand had been unpleasant of course, she was unable to knit, and that to Hilda, was the worst punishment of all. One fellow prisoner had tried to bully Hilda, thinking that this white haired elderly lady would be an easy target. Hilda had looked her in the eye, informed her that she was here for killing five old men, and that not only would killing a woman be a different experience for her, it would be good to make it the round half dozen. There had been something in Hilda's face which had warned the woman to leave her alone. She had backed off, blustering that she had respect for the aged and wouldn't demean herself by touching Hilda. After that, Hilda had been shunned. She didn't care. She didn't wish to mix with the hoi polloi, the junkies, the drug dealers, the shoplifters, she was a cut above them. In her own mind, she was queen of the prison.

She had been taken to the Crown Court where she had plead guilty, smiling benignly at the red robed judge as if he was bestowing some special honour on her. She had been remanded for further reports. Once back in the van returning her and sundry other miserable souls to the prison, Hilda had sat in the small cell like compartment, partially resigned to her fate. She would just have to make the best of it, and see what happened. Hilda was something of a fatalist. Idly she rubbed her wrists. The custody guard had removed her handcuffs. This was strictly against the rules, but he was young, inexperienced in the ways of the world, and he thought Hilda looked a bit like his old grandmother. He took pity on her, and slipped the cuffs off her wrists with a cheeky,

"There you go Granny, you be a good girl now, and I'll come back when we are nearly there. Don't want either of us to get into trouble, do we?"

Hilda had scowled at him, furious at being called "Granny", and gratitude certainly couldn't be counted as one of her weaknesses. The young man withdrew, feeling a bit peeved that his generous gesture had been met with such a lack of appreciation, but too green to renege and too embarrassed to refasten the handcuffs.

They were only a mile or so from the court when the accident happened. A double decker bus careered down the hill, its brakes having failed disastrously, it crossed the junction and hit the side of the prison van with a terrific impact. Police and ambulances had rushed to the scene, and in the chaos and confusion, Hilda Hopkins picked herself up from the floor, limped into the crowd, and melted away.

There had been a restaurant overlooking the crash scene. Many of the patrons had left their tables and were clustered round the windows and door, gazing out at the scene of devastation. Hilda walked into the restaurant, gathered up two unattended handbags and a raincoat and sneaked out through the kitchen. She walked down the entry and ducked into a doorway. She slipped the coat on, it was a little long, Hilda was not a tall woman, and she had lost nearly two stones of weight while she had been on remand, but it wasn't noticeably the wrong size. Thankfully almost anything went these days. She quickly rifled through the handbags, the cash went into her pocket, the credit cards regretfully she left behind, there was no trace of the pin numbers with these ones. One handbag contained an oyster travel card. Hilda smiled, that would be useful to get her away from here. The rest of the contents were just the minutiae of any woman's bag, make up, pens, a diary, paper tissues, tampons nothing of any particular use to Hilda. She stepped out and tossed the bags into a nearby dumpster, and headed towards the road at the end of the lane.

It was quieter here, everyone who had been in the area had evidently hurried to the scene of the accident. Hilda started walking down the road in the opposite direction until she saw the round circular sign for the Underground. She went down into the ticket hall and used the stolen oyster card at the barrier, it worked. After a short uneventful journey Hilda came up the escalator into Waterloo Station and eagerly scanned the departures board. She needed to get to Danemouth. The last time she had been there, she had buried several hundred pounds in one of the chines, a long narrow valley leading down to the sea, and hopefully it would still be there.

Hilda had obstinately refused to disclose what she had done with all the money she had stolen from her gentlemen's accounts. She had simply declared that she had spent it all. There was a train scheduled to depart in ten minutes going to Southhurst on Sea. Danemouth was three stops before there. This was a slow train which look liked it was scheduled to stop just about everywhere on the route. Hilda scanned the board again, the express didn't go for another fifty minutes. She started walking towards the ticket office mulling over possibilities in her mind. An extra forty minutes here might be dangerous. It would be best to get right away as soon as possible. Hilda stopped by a self service machine. She would buy a ticket from this, that way the ticket seller would have no reason to remember her. Not that anyone did take much notice of her anyway, she thought resentfully. Look at what she'd done, and none of these idiots, she looked round scornfully at the hurrying passengers, had any idea who she was. She dug into her coat pocket and fed notes and coins into the machine. She clasped the little orange ticket in her hand, and walked confidently towards the platform.

Hilda was safely installed in a corner seat in the carriage. She had found a discarded magazine and held it up in front of her face as the train slowly moved away from the platform. She saw two uniformed policemen walking through the entrance, glancing around as they made their way through the station. Was it a normal patrol, or something extra? Hilda bit her lip, were they looking for her here specifically, or were all the London Stations being targeted? She supposed she must have been missed by now, after all, she was an important fugitive, heads would roll if she wasn't caught soon. Would they guess she would make for Danemouth? The wheels hummed as the train picked up speed. Well, whatever, she was stuck on here for now, she would just have to see what transpired.

Chapter 2

The train took the best part of two hours to get to Danemouth. Hilda sat and fretted at each stop, half expecting the Transport Police to come on board and search amongst the passengers. Nobody in uniform had appeared, other than the ticket inspector, and he had punched her ticket without even glancing at her. Passengers had alighted and new ones had settled down for the journey. Hilda had watched the woman across the aisle from her. She had got on at Basington, dumping her suitcase in the rack behind her before settling down with a laptop and working from some papers, totally engrossed. Hilda wished she had something to do. She had read the magazine through twice and wasn't inclined to peruse it a third time.

The train slowed, it was coming into Danemouth. Hilda stood up, wrapping the overlarge raincoat across her front and made her way to the door. As the train came into the platform she glimpsed two uniformed officers just the other side of the ticket barrier. She turned away from the door and slipped into the adjacent toilet, heart thumping. One of the officers had stepped across to say something to his colleague, otherwise Hilda would have been off the train before she spotted them. Were they there because she had originally been apprehended in Danemouth, was it a coincidence, or was every station throughout the land staked out? Hilda staggered as the train started its journey again. She fell against the wall, and grimaced. She hadn't escaped entirely unscathed from the collision, she was bruised all down her left side.

She eased the door open, but stayed at the end of the carriage. The ticket inspector would be along soon to check the new passengers' tickets. Hilda's ticket only took her as far as Danemouth, she didn't want a fuss being made. She peered along the carriage, sure enough, the man was on his way. She slipped back into the toilet. She sat there for some time, debating whether to risk going back into the carriage. She felt the train slowing down again. She squeezed her eyes shut trying to visualise the names on the destination board. This must be Grimes Cove. Would they have police here, or was it too small a place for them to bother about? Strangers here would stand out like a sore thumb she guessed. Hilda made a split second decision. She slipped out of the toilet, quietly removed the suitcase belonging to her diligent fellow passenger, and as the train stopped, opened the door and manoeuvred the case down the steps behind her.

The doors slammed shut and the train disappeared round a bend in the track. Hilda studied the layout of the station. It was just a Halt, with a platform either side of the track, and an iron bridge spanning the two. Behind Hilda there was a small wicket gate, she pushed her way through it and emerged into the main street of the small coastal village.

Hilda was hungry. The train fare had been expensive, even second class single, and had eaten into her small hoard of cash. She thought longingly of all the money stashed in Danemouth; still she had been wise not to alight there. By now she would have been back at that awful Police Station. She could smell fish and chips. Her mouth salivated. She could afford a hot meal, she needed it, and she had to build up her strength.

She sat on a seat in a shelter on the seafront eating her meal out of its paper wrapping. It was divine, especially after her diet of prison food. The chips were plump, slathered in salt and vinegar, while the tender white flesh of the fish was crisply coated in a batter which simply melted in her mouth. She ate greedily, interspersing her meal with sips of Dandelion and Burdock from a can. Eventually there was no more left, she screwed up the paper and stuffed it behind the seat. The empty can, squashed flat under her foot, was kicked out of the way too. Now what? She hunted through her pockets. She had twenty pounds and sixty two pence in total. That wouldn't get her very far. She doubted it would even pay for a night's lodging.

How far away was Danemouth she wondered? If the Police were watching the stations, maybe she could slip in unobserved from the coast road. She looked at the suitcase she had stolen. Initially she had taken it as camouflage, she had thought it would have looked less odd for a train passenger to be pulling a suitcase along, it made her look more like a normal visitor. She was stuck with the damn thing now though, she didn't want to leave any sort of a trail behind her. Sighing, she pulled up the handle and started walking along the coast road, dragging the thing behind her on wobbly wheels. You would have thought, she reflected bitterly, that a business woman like that would have had something a bit more upmarket so far as luggage was concerned.

She thought about the fine red tartan case she had had when she had been on the ill-fated excursion to Danemouth. Now that had looked smart. She wondered briefly if Susan Morris had kept it, or if it had been returned to the catalogue shop, or just destroyed as unwanted evidence? Hilda had purchased it using Susan Morris' credit card, along with a wardrobe of stunning clothes and an expensive coach excursion.

Chapter 3

The light had faded, and it had started to rain. Once Hilda left the confines of the village and started to walk along the coastal path she felt the wind rising, blowing the rain into her face. There was no hood on the raincoat and her hair quickly became soaked. Her side was aching. There was nothing broken, thankfully, she was only bruised, but she must be black and blue under her clothes.

Ahead of her Hilda caught sight of a light amongst some trees. She gravitated towards it. There was no way she would be able to walk into Danemouth tonight. She was cold, wet, sore, and very, very tired. The light proved to belong to a fair sized house set back on the cliff top amongst a small copse of pine trees. Hilda stood at the gate and surveyed the building. It looked desolate, the wood needed painting, and the light filtering out through the fanlight above the door was struggling against the grime smeared across the glass. A sign by the gate proclaimed that this was the "Travellers' Rest Guesthouse". Another sign in the downstairs window advised "Vacancies". This was flanked by a card reading "Help Required".

Hilda stood there, water streaming down her face, and contemplated the two signs. They had vacancies, but she doubted if even here twenty pounds would go very far. They also needed help. That probably meant a chambermaid or something similar. Well, housework was one thing Hilda was good at, that and machine knitting. The machine knitting wouldn't be much use here, but she wasn't afraid of hard work. She could probably get away with taking five years or so off her age, but what about national insurance numbers and such like..... Maybe she could stall for a couple of weeks, if they took her on that is, then just quietly disappear one day when the hue and cry had calmed down a bit. Hilda shivered. She wanted to go and hammer at the front door, but her native cunning had kicked in. She had been so astute to get this far, she had to continue planning her way, no point in getting caught at this stage of the game.

Why would she be wanting a job at her age? What was her name, she could hardly call herself Hilda Hopkins, but nothing too complicated. She needed to be able to remember who she was supposed to be. She was recently widowed, she had lost her house, she had no kin, nowhere to go, but she was willing to work for bed and board. That would do. Name? She liked her name, Hilda was old English, it was a strong name. So something similar, Hilary, that was close enough. And what about her surname? Her maiden name had been Sheepshanks. She had endured years of torment about that, plus it was a little unusual, it might arouse comment. Her face cleared, how about Wolfe, a wolf in sheepshanks' clothing, she giggled, her ingenuity amazed herself sometimes.

Hilda marched up to the door and banged on the knocker. It took a while for the door to be opened. First of all she heard shuffling footsteps, a clinking sound followed as a chain was removed. The door creaked open, unoiled hinges shrieking in protest. A woman stood there, feet firmly planted on the shabby, scratched linoleum. She was a little older than Hilda, around the same height, and her scrawny figure was topped with a mass of grey hair scragged back into a bun. Behind her the dingy passage led to the foot of a flight of stairs. These were partly covered by a carpet runner, originally patterned in gold and beige but now faded to a muddy brown, and even from this distance Hilda could see the dust on the wooden risers.

"It says help wanted," stated Hilda with no preamble, "and I'm unemployed. Will I suit?"

"I dare say you might. You'd best come in," replied the woman ungraciously, holding the door a little wider, "let's have a look at you."

Hilda bumped the suitcase over the door jamb and entered the lobby. A stale smell of old cabbage lingered in the air. A door marked "Lounge" opened and an elderly man peered out. He bore an uncanny resemblance to a tortoise popping out of its shell.

"Not your business Mr Lancaster" snapped the woman and the man withdrew his head sharply.

The woman pointed to a small dining room.

"In here, sit yourself down."

Hilda sat gratefully enough, she was so tired. The woman disappeared into the kitchen and reappeared with a towel which she silently handed to Hilda. It had once been white, but was now a dingy grey. Hilda rubbed it over her head, and dried her face.

"Abigail Moffat, Mrs" said the woman, "I'm the proprietor of this establishment."

Abigail? Hilda felt a jolt of surprise. Abigail had been the name of the pretty porcelain doll she had kept in her bedroom for years. Was this a lucky omen?

"Hilary Wolfe," replied Hilda, pulling herself together, "also a Mrs, but I'm widowed."

"Same here. So why do you want a job? You look a bit long in the tooth to be starting a new career, I'd have had you down as a potential guest."

Hilda went into her story, recently widowed, homeless, most of the pension had died with her husband, she wanted to live by the seaside and if necessary, she would work for bed and board.

Abigail Moffat sat back and regarded her intently. Hilda strove to keep her own gaze steady.

"I'll give you a weeks' trial, see if you suit, see if you can manage the work. Doubt I'll get anybody else all the way out here anyway. Bed and board and thirty pounds cash in hand. No need to worry the tax man about our business, unless you want to pay contributions of course?"

Hilda felt her shoulders sag with relief,

"That would be excellent, Mrs Moffat," better be respectful, she thought, even though she could probably run rings round this old biddy. Better show some interest too.

"How many bedrooms are there?"

"Two doubles, two singles for the guests on the first floor. The doubles are ensuite, the singles share a bathroom. There's a lounge, this dining room, and my quarters. I have a sitting room and a bedroom, my man's dead too these three years. There's the kitchen, and you can have the small room at the top of the house, you'll have to share the guests' bathroom but we don't get many guests, not along here."

Hilda looked surprised.

"it's a bit too far from the village, a bit too close to the top of the cliffs, gets all the bad weather and I can't afford all the mod cons. There's a TV in the lounge, not in the rooms, although I've got a black and white portable you can put in your room for now", she conceded gracefully, "I won't want you mixing in the Lounge with any guests we do get."

Hilda inclined her head. Good, the less access people had to the news broadcasts and to her the better.

"I've got a Mr Lancaster staying here. He's not so much a guest as a fixture, came about eight months ago, and pays by the month. He's got one of the single rooms. There was a couple here last week." her mouth turned down at the corners, "unmarried of course. They think I can't tell, just here for a bit of rumpty pumpty on the side. I would have liked to tell them to sling their hooks, but you know how it is when business is slow."

Hilda nodded her head gently as if she understood perfectly. Mrs Moffat led the way upstairs, Hilda followed, bumping the suitcase in her wake. The room was small. There was a single bed, a wardrobe, a chair and a table. The whole place was covered in dust, and the old cabbage smell had even pervaded up here.

"There's bed linen in the airing cupboard next to the bathroom on the floor below," said Mrs Moffat, "I'll see you in the morning, Hilary, half six."

"I get Hilly for short," murmured Hilda.

"Half past six Hilary, in the kitchen."

Chapter 4

"Have you seen the News?" Claire Naylor stopped by a table in the Police Canteen. Barbara Grey was looking at a set of family photographs belonging to her team colleague, Clive Barcroft. He had just returned from a weeks' holiday at a holiday camp with his wife, Lillian and their two children. Barbara had had something of a schoolgirl crush on Barcroft a few months ago. As she gazed at the happy little family beaming from the photographs she was glad she had kept her feelings hidden and hadn't made a fool of herself.

"No," replied Barcroft, "what's caught your interest, Sarge?"

"Remember the Hopkins woman?"

Barbara Grey jumped and the photographs scattered across the table.

"As if I'd ever forget, what's she done now, Sarge?"

"She absconded on her way back to prison yesterday afternoon."

"Absconded?" Barbara looked at the Detective Sergeant blankly as her fingers automatically patted the photographs into order before sliding them back into their envelope.

"Escaped, run off, scarpered..." replied Naylor.

"I know what absconded means," Barbara replied irritably, "I meant how did it happen? She must be pushing eighty by now."

Detective Sergeant Naylor laughed, "Oh she's nowhere near that age Barbara, and you know it! No, it seems the custody van crashed, and she simply walked away. A bus hit it, full of passengers, apparently there was a fair bit of confusion at the scene. Lots of injured, some walking, some not."

"And no-one noticed an old woman wandering around in handcuffs?" This from Clive Barcroft.

"Apparently the guard had removed them, thought she would be more comfortable, said she looked like his old Granny."

Barbara Grey raised her eyes to the ceiling.

"Ye gods, what are they recruiting these days, Boy Scouts? Let's get back to the old days when they used prison officers as escorts, at least they knew the sort of thing they were dealing with. A harmless old Granny? I think not. In fact let me amend that, I know not. How's your toe, Sarge?"

Claire Naylor grimaced. When Hilda Hopkins had been apprehended she had dropped a large, heavy ribber weight on Claire's toe. The toe had been fractured, and it had taken several weeks to mend. Claire reckoned it still twinged when there was rain in the air.

"So where do they believe she is?" interrupted Barcroft.

"Dunno, she's melted out of sight. She won't be coming back here I don't suppose. All her stuff is in storage and her house is boarded up. She could be anywhere, still in London perhaps. I don't know what she will do for food or transport, she wouldn't have had any money on her."

"Maybe she has an account under another name. She pinched thousands from her lodgers, and I don't believe she spent it all in a week, no matter what she said during the interviews," Barbara commented.

"Well she was stuck in Neston until the Tuesday," Claire Naylor frowned as she struggled to recall the finer details of the case, "And there's no bank there. Just one of those hole in the wall machines which charge you for removing your own money."

Claire and her partner Colin were saving for a mortgage deposit, and Claire bitterly resented any unnecessary inroads into her cash flow.

"Then," she continued, "She was on that coach excursion. I can't remember the particulars, I know they visited a couple of Stately Homes to look at the House and gardens and they had a stay in Danemouth before going on to more Houses and back to Midchester. It was advertised as a Circular Tour. We caught the Hopkins woman at Danemouth, so she dipped out on the remainder of the trip. Got a free ride in a police car instead."

"And didn't she pal up with some woman on the trip?" asked Barbara, "funny name, Cress, Radish......"

"Lettice. Yes you're right Barbara, maybe we'll go and have a chat with her, see if she remembers Hopkins visiting any banks, or even leaving anything with her."

Chapter 5

Hilda looked round the small bedroom. This would suit very well. She ran her finger along the table and regarded the trail left in the dust. It looked like the whole place needed a lot of elbow grease expended on it. Good job she wasn't afraid of hard work, plus she had many innovations of her own when it came to cleaning products, gleaned from sundry television programmes. Lots of lemon juice, vinegar, borax and baking powder, never mind fancy detergents, she would make this place shine, and the Moffat woman would be forced to keep her on.

She looked at the suitcase on the bed. Better have a look inside, see what there was. She rooted around the contents; it was mainly clothes, plus a sponge bag containing soap, toothbrush and toothpaste, and a romantic novel. Hilda's lip curled. She had no interest whatsoever in romance. Despite what she had told Mrs Moffat, she did have a husband somewhere, and so far as she knew he could still be alive. He had deserted her years ago.

There was also a pair of slippers. Hilda tried them on, they were a size too big and flip flopped as she took a few steps, but she could always stuff the toes with tissue. Hilda pulled out the clothes, and held a blouse against her body. It didn't look too bad a fit. She tried it on. The buttons strained across her chest but it would do for the time being. There were two fine knit jumpers, they too were a very snug fit, but just about wearable. One skirt was useless, far too tight, but there were a couple of summer skirts with elasticated waistbands which Hilda managed to squeeze into. What a good job she had lost some weight in prison, she thought, otherwise she would never have been able to use any of this other than the slippers. It was much different in films she thought, sourly. The six foot tall slim hero would knock out the uniformed five foot eight chunky bad guy, and the bad guy's outfit would fit the hero as if it had been tailor-made for him! Maybe Mrs Moffat had some work overalls, if so Hilda would be able to muddle through until she was paid and could get a proper change of clothes.

Thankfully Mrs Moffat did have a good supply of the wraparound type of apron, and Hilda had gratefully accepted three of these. They hid her ill fitting clothes perfectly, without constricting her as she went about her duties. Mrs Moffat, while not exactly fulsome with praise, seemed satisfied with her efforts, and as the first week drew to its close, Hilda felt hopeful that she had found a secure hideaway.

She awoke early on Sunday morning to the sound of traffic passing her window. She looked at the clock. Half past seven. Mr Lancaster didn't have his breakfast until half past nine on a Sunday, or so Mrs Moffat had informed her, therefore Sunday was a chance to have a lie in. Hilda got up, briefly washed and dressed and slipped downstairs. The sound of all the activity had alarmed her, there had scarcely been any traffic passing the place at all during the week she had been there.

Mrs Moffat was up. She had been drinking a cup of coffee in the kitchen and came through into the lobby, still holding the drink, to see who was there.

"They have a car boot sale just down the road on that big field," explained Mrs Moffat, seeing Hilda looking out of the front window watching the cars lumbering past. "It finishes in October, then starts again next March. Bit of a nuisance unless you like that sort of thing."

Hilda said she would like to go and have a wander round. She was keen on visiting car boot sales.

"You can go at eleven, I won't miss you for a couple of hours then," conceded Mrs Moffat, "best time for bargains too, the booters are desperate to get rid of the stuff."

Hilda had worn her long raincoat. She found a felt beret that had been left behind by a previous visitor and covered her head with most of that. She hadn't been paid yet, but she still had the twenty pounds and sixty-two pence in her pockets. She had to fork out 50 pence just to get into the sale, but she was pleased to see that it was well attended, there were several lanes of cars, while quite a few large vans were parked on the perimeter.

She bought some second hand clothes, nothing spectacular but at least they would fit her better than the ones she had, and a shoulder bag. She had felt lost without a handbag to her name. On one stall she found knitting needles and purchased a carrier bag full of yarn oddments to go with them for a pound. Brilliant, she could start knitting again. She tramped around the lanes, carrying her two bulging bags fascinated by the variety of objects on sale. The day was dry, if a little cool, the wind wasn't as vicious down here as it was around the headland. Hilda began to thoroughly enjoy herself. The fresh air and the exercise had brought colour to her cheeks, banishing the last traces of prison pallor. She would just have a quick look at the vans at the end, then she really must get back to Travellers' Rest. She had to stay in Mrs Moffat's good books.

Ahead of her a van had a sign on its side declaring "House Clearances". Not very interesting, thought Hilda, looking at the motley collection of furniture, crockery and books. She glanced at the back of the van and her heart skipped a beat. She recognised the shape of a knitting machine. She scuttled forward and looked at it, reading the name on the case. It was the same make as the one she had had back in Merrydown Crescent, but this was a later model, even better. She put her bags down, laid the machine on the ground and opened it up. There was a carriage, and the yarn mast, but no accessories case. Still it would be a start. She pursed her lips as she looked at the needle bed, it was sticky with oil and grime. But she wanted it. She caught the eye of the man sitting in the driver's seat.

"How much?"

"Fifteen quid love."

Hilda just about had that amount on her, but she decided to haggle, nothing ventured, nothing gained.

"It's pretty filthy. Does it work? Seems a bit steep, fifteen quid. I only have my pension."

The man considered. Hilda's was the first enquiry he had had for the machine, and he had brought the thing to several car boot sales.

`"Give us an offer then."

"Five pounds," replied Hilda cheekily.

The man guffawed,

"I'll do the jokes round here love. You can have it for ten quid if you like?"

Hilda liked, and handed over a ten pound note. She only had a few pounds in change now, she hoped she would get her cash in hand soon.

She clicked the top back onto the case, and lifted it up. It was heavy. She hadn't seen any table clamps in with it either, that would be a nuisance. It needed to be anchored firmly to a surface when she was knitting on it.

"Hang on love," said the man, suddenly remembering something.

Hilda looked up sharply, surely the man wasn't going to renege on the deal. He had her money after all. He had started rummaging in the back of the van, and pulled out a plastic carrier bag crammed with small boxes.

"There's this as well, you might as well take the lot."

He thrust the carrier bag into her arms. Hilda inspected it curiously. She could see a machine accessories box, and sundry other boxes, and a roll of punch card all stuffed into the bag. She was so pleased she gave the man a look of genuine gratitude. He threw a black plastic rubbish sack towards her.

"Might be easier if you shove all your bags into that. Have you got far to go?"

"No, just to…" Hilda's natural caution kicked in, "just to the car park, thanks."

It had been a struggle. Knitting machines aren't light things to carry any distance, but sheer enthusiasm seemed to give Hilda extra strength and she arrived back triumphantly with all her booty. She had to take everything up to her room in two lots. Quickly she tipped out the carrier bag the man had given her onto the counterpane. The accessory box was full, there were clamps, transfer tools even some ravel cord. She had magic cams too, and the right and left stops to go with them. Hilda grinned. She picked up a box, "Linker", great, she'd always wanted a linker, this would be quicker than doing latch tool cast offs. A long thin box contained an automatic weaving arm. Hilda had never bothered much with weaving techniques, she felt it took too long, moving the yarn from side to side on each row. She would explore the possibilities of this thing though. Another box produced a rib carriage transfer tool. That wasn't much use to her just yet, the machine was a single bed one, but maybe sometime in the future she could buy a ribber? There was a packet of basic punch cards. Hilda went through them, seventeen out of the original twenty, never mind, that was enough to be going on with. There was also a small roll of blank punch card. And that was it, no punch for making the holes in the punch cards, so she wouldn't be able to design her own just yet, and no wool winder. Well she didn't have any wool anyway, apart from the balls she had bought along with her knitting needles, and being hand double knitting that was a bit too thick for this machine as it was standard gauge, and not a chunky one. She took the lid off the machine. It would have to be deep cleaned, all the old oil and fluff removed and the needles checked.

Hilda took the latch tool and poked its handle into the side of the machine, until the sponge bar protruded at the other end. She carefully eased it part of the way out. The sponge had deteriorated and there was no spring left in it at all. First priority then, a new sponge bar, that would make all the difference. If only she dared go into Danemouth. It was one of the few places left in the south which had a shop that catered for machine knitters. Hilda remembered seeing a stall at the Knitting Machine Exhibition advertising their wares.

"Hilary, do you intend doing any work today?"

Hilda frowned as Mrs Moffat's reedy voice rang up the stairs. Keep her sweet, she thought, you've dropped in lucky here Hilda my girl, bed, board and now my lovely, lovely knitting machine. Or it will be lovely once I've seen to it.

"Coming straight away, Mrs Moffat. Sorry, forgot the time."

Hilda had found her niche. The first three weeks passed quickly, and she found that she had made herself indispensable in the guest house. Hilda had started at the front door, carefully cleaning the fanlight so that the light streamed through it and beams of colour danced on the scuffed linoleum, and worked her way through the whole house, apart from Mrs Moffat's private quarters of course, with mop, bucket, hoover, and dusters. At her instigation the lace curtains had been taken down, soaked overnight in whitener, and replaced shining snowy white rather than drab grey. The dining room had been scrubbed from top to bottom, all the windows had been cleaned then prized open for the rough wind which buffeted the headland to sweep through the house, pushing the smell of old cabbage out before it. The place gleamed inside. Outside it still needed a lick of paint, but Hilda felt that was something which was beyond her.

All they needed now were some guests. It was hardly the place for passing trade. Most of the visitors to Grimes Cove stayed in the village itself. It was low season now too, so there wasn't a surfeit of guests to be sent along the coastal road to Travellers' Rest. They had Mr Lancaster of course. He was definitely a fixture in the place. Hilda had to share the bathroom with him, much to her chagrin because the man was a slob.

Chapter 6

Claire Naylor rang the bell of the neat townhouse and stepped back to look along the avenue. It all looked very quiet and peaceful, it was the sort of area that estate agents advertised as "respectable."

The door opened and a middle aged mousey looking woman looked out enquiringly.

"Miss Lettice Leverson," asked Claire, although she had already recognised the woman from the original enquiry. She flashed her warrant card, "Police, I wonder if we could have a word, please?"

Miss Leverson stepped back, her hands fluttering at her breast like small birds.

"What about?" she glanced back into the house, "I don't want Mother to be disturbed."

"We are just pursuing some enquiries," smiled Claire, "we won't disturb your mother, it's you we'd like to speak to."

Claire moved forward confidently, and Miss Leverson stepped back into the hall.

There was a whirring sound, and an old lady seated in an electric wheelchair appeared in a doorway behind Miss Leverson.

"Lettice! What is happening? Who are these people, why have you let them in? If they are Jehovah's Witnesses you can tell them we are Anglican."

"It's the Police, Mother," replied Miss Leverson diffidently.

"The Police, at my door? What have you been up to Lettice? You haven't been shoplifting?"

"Mother!" Miss Leverson sounded genuinely aggrieved, "of course not. How could you?"

"We would just like a word with your daughter Mrs Leverson about a person she was briefly acquainted with a few months ago. She was on the same coach excursion as your daughter."

"I always said no good comes of gadding about," the old woman muttered wrathfully, "if you had been here, in your proper place Lettice none of this would have happened."

She turned her head and looked at Claire through small black piggy eyes, "You, young woman, did you come in a police car?"

"Yes," replied Claire, "a plain one, it doesn't have stripes and the word police down the side."

"Let's be thankful for small mercies. You'd better come in and ask what you need to. The sooner you ask, the sooner you can go. Young man!"

DC Graham Perkins looked up sharply, he was lounging against the front door.

"Don't lean against the door, it doesn't need you to hold it up, and there will be trouble if you mark it."

To his eternal shame, Perkins found himself responding to the authority in Mrs Leverson's voice. He straightened up immediately, blushing like a naughty schoolboy.

Mrs Leverson had backed into the sitting room. Lettice gave her a frustrated look, but it seemed that Mrs Leverson was determined to be present during the interview.

"We really would like to speak to Lettice on her own," Claire insisted firmly.

"I'm not being evicted from my own sitting room," snapped Mrs Leverson. "Lettice, take these people into the kitchen, and be mindful, it's nearly time for my elevenses. I shall get palpitations if I'm upset, you know that."

"Yes Mother," Lettice smiled ruefully at Claire and Perkins and ushered them through to a cosy kitchen at the rear of the house.

They sat round the kitchen table. Lettice had offered them a glass of lemonade each which they had accepted. Claire felt it would go some way to helping Lettice become less anxious, she seemed to be a woman who was more relaxed when she had something to do.

"I'm sorry about Mother," she said, "she gets so impatient being stuck in that wheelchair, she was always such an active woman."

"No worries," replied Claire, giving the frightened woman a warm smile, "we just wanted to speak to you about Hilda Hopkins, she was on your coach when you did the Circular Tour around Danemouth, she passed herself off as Hilda Morris."

"Oh, Hilly, it was Hilary, not Hilda. Yes, she was a bit odd, but we were both on our own so we sort of gravitated together. Mother didn't like it when she heard what she had done, she said I must have been very credulous not to realise the woman was a mass murderer."

"She fooled a lot of people. You really mustn't blame yourself for not realising," Claire said gently, "it's a lot easier to spot the signs with hindsight."

"I suppose so. But what do you want to know? We only sat next to each other on the coach, and did a bit of shopping together. I had to buy postcards at each place we stopped, Mother wouldn't like it if she didn't get her daily postcard."

Lettice was looking anxious again.

"Did you ever see her going into a bank, or a building society, or even the Post Office? We're wondering if she had any opportunity to open a new savings account or something similar you see?"

Lettice screwed up her face in concentration.

"We went round some of the Houses together, and we went shopping but we only went to that big newsagent's chain, I had to buy a postcard and it seemed to be the best place, and then we went into a tearoom for tea and cakes. That I think was the Thursday, and on Friday we did another couple of Houses and Gardens and we arrived at the Grand Hotel in Danemouth on the Friday evening in time for dinner. The banks would have been closed by then, so no, I don't think she ever did."

Claire was quite impressed with Lettice's recall, but then, she supposed, she doubted if the woman had much excitement or change in the tedium of her life looking after Mother.

"There was Saturday morning. Quite a few places open on a Saturday now don't they? I went off to the Aquarium, Hilly said she wanted to look at the antique shops I think, I seem to remember her saying she only liked her fish fried or something. It was a joke, she didn't make many jokes, it surprised me. But she seemed to be very excited that day."

"She'd made plans to go to a Machine Knitting Exhibition," explained Graham, "it seems to have been a passion of hers, knitting, she was probably thinking about that."

"Oh, I quite like knitting too," replied Lettie, "it's very soothing. I would have liked one of those knitting machines too, but Mother said no, she wouldn't like the noise when it was being used. It would give her a headache."

"Hilda Hopkins had made herself a small workroom," said Claire, she thought this house must have spare rooms, it was a big house for just two women, "I'm sure your mother wouldn't notice any noise if you were in a different room. I saw one of those machines in use at the Show when we caught Hopkins, they don't make that much racket you know. If you are keen on knitting, you should really consider getting one and putting it somewhere quiet, it would give you an interest."

"Do you think so? Mother doesn't really like it if I go against her wishes, but I could make some pretty shawls and things for her I suppose, she might like that. And I could even join a club too. Oh sorry, that's not what you are asking is it? No, I don't remember Hilly going to any banks, unless as I say she did it on Saturday morning."

She sat there, looking like an expectant spaniel waiting for a biscuit.

"And she didn't give you anything to look after for her?"

"Oh no. Mother said I must always pack my own case, and never offer to carry anything for anyone else. Mother saw this programme about the Bangkok Hilton, apparently it was full of women who had done favours for their boy friends, carrying talcum powder tins which turned out to be drugs. I don't have a boy friend, Mother says it wouldn't be suitable at my age, but she was very insistent when I went on holiday that I mustn't get involved with anyone or do anything for them. And she's right too. I only sat next to this Hilda Hopkins woman and I had to give a statement when it all happened and she got caught. It was lucky she pleaded Guilty, if I had had to appear in Court as a witness I don't know what would have happened. Mother certainly wouldn't have liked it, she was vocal enough as it was."

Lettice gave a small shiver as she relived the episode.

Claire stood up, motioning towards Graham to stand also.

"You've been very helpful Miss Leverson, cleared up a few questions for us, we are very grateful."

Lettice smiled shyly, she showed the two officers out, glancing fearfully at the sitting room door as she did so.

"Think about that knitting machine," Claire said cheerfully, "it would give you an interest, and an excuse to get out and about a bit."

She settled into the passenger seat in the car, and pulled the seat belt across her chest, fumbling with the buckle. Graham slid into the driving seat and switched on the engine.

"Do you think she will?" he asked.

"Will what?"

"Get one of those infernal machines?"

"They're not infernal. I was amazed when I was at that Exhibition to see just what could be made on one of them. I'm toying with the idea of getting one for myself actually. As to our Lettice," she grimaced, "I don't really see her as a rebel Graham. She might desperately want something like that, but I doubt she will ever pluck up the courage to go out and buy one, Mother wouldn't like it!"

Chapter 7

Hilda battled her way along the cliff top. The wind screamed around here even when it was a tranquil day in the Cove below. She had awoken with a splitting headache. She had taken two paracetamol, and Mrs Moffat had suggested that she went out for a ten minutes walk to clear her head.

Hilda decided she would go down to the beach. She hadn't ventured down there yet. There was a small path which wound its way down to the Cove. The side of the cliff was quite steep. Hilda didn't much care for heights, but she could cope with them if she had to. She had only managed to get a hundred yards or so of the way down when she slipped and skidded on the muddy path. Hilda was terrified, she tried to keep her balance but she could not get a grip on the slippery ground. All of a sudden she sprawled onto her face and rolled towards the corner of the path. She was brought up short by a clump of gorse bushes. The whole area was dotted with gorse, not one of Hilda's favourite plants, but on this occasion she embraced it, literally, squealing as the thorns cut into her hands.

She scrambled behind the gorse bush, pushing her way in between the thick trunks to try and use the cliff face to pull herself upright. Moments later she felt herself falling again. Not far, she dropped onto her knees, then sprawled forward onto solid ground. Badly winded, Hilda lay there for several minutes, before rolling over onto her back. She could see daylight filtering through leaves obstructing an opening. She sat up and tried to look over her shoulder, but the inky blackness defeated her.

Hilda crawled across to the entrance, and used the wall to haul herself up. She pushed her way back through the gorse bushes onto the path. The cave's entrance was completely hidden. Hilda climbed painfully back up to the cliff top and made her way across to the guesthouse. An idea was germinating in her mind. She took a large black torch out of the kitchen drawer, and quietly let herself out of the back door.

This time she went down the path very carefully, and arrived unscathed at the bend in the path. She squeezed behind the bushes, and flashed the torch through the opening. The cave wasn't particularly big. It was roughly spherical in shape and the floor was rough and uneven. Hilda went all round, but there were no other entrances to other caves, it was just a hole in the cliff. She passed the beam of the torch backwards and forwards across the floor. There was no debris, no rubbish, no sign that the cave was ever used by children or adults. She knew there were more caves along the coast, but they were nearer the beach. They had been used by smugglers years ago, but this one had apparently been overlooked.

Hilda went back up the path and returned the torch to its place. Mrs Moffat clicked her tongue in irritation when she saw the state of Hilda's clothes.

"I slipped on the path," Hilda explained sulkily, "I didn't do it on purpose, I'll go and get changed."

She took her clean clothes and slipped into the front double guest bedroom. Hilda had started using the ensuite facilities whenever the room was empty, which was most of the time, rather than her own bathroom which she had to share with Mr Lancaster. The man was a health hazard. He never wiped the sink or the bath after he had used it. Hilda was also harbouring deep suspicions about what else he used the sink for.

She showered quickly, her mind full of the possibilities surrounding her new find. The cave would make a glorious bolt hole if the police ever came calling. It had been some time now since her escape, she had faded from the news and the newspapers many weeks ago, but, she thought complacently, even though she was much cleverer than the police, it would do no harm to be prepared. She would get a sleeping bag, put in a supply of bottled water, some tins of food, and a tin opener of course, and what else. A bucket and a roll of loo paper, she wrinkled her nose, but the basics had to be seen to. A torch, plus batteries, it was going to be a veritable shopping list by the time she finished. But as things turned out, the cave was destined to be put to another use.

Chapter 8

Hilda sat up in her bed with a start. She looked round her room. The moon glinted off the mast of her knitting machine. She really must screw up her courage and go to the knitting and sewing shop in Danemouth and buy a new sponge bar. The machine was gleaming since she had cleaned it, a new sponge bar and it would be as near to new as it would ever be. Then there would be no stopping her, she would be able to knit to her heart's content.   There was another muffled thump. Hilda strained her ears, she could hear the faintest of sounds from downstairs, as if something was bumping along the passage leading to the lobby. Hilda slid out of bed and pattered down the plain wooden stairs which led from her room to the guests' floor. She peered over the banister rail in time to see a pair of feet slithering along the floor towards the dining room.

Hilda stepped onto the top step, and let out a strangled squeak as her feet shot out from beneath her. She sat down hard on the landing, wincing as pain shot through her ample backside. That bloody top stair, she thought, the one with the dodgy stair rail. She had told Mrs Moffat several times the stairs were a death trap, she really needed to get a man in to fit a proper stair carpet. This runner with the rusty rails had been an accident waiting to happen.

Hilda hauled herself up, and padded carefully but quietly down the stairs, rubbing her hand across her sore bottom. She peeped round the dining room door. The feet had belonged to Mr Lancaster, the permanent guest, and it was Mrs Moffat who was hauling his lifeless body along in fits and starts.

Hilda stepped forward and picked up the man's body by his legs.

"Where to?" she hissed.

Mrs Moffat looked at her ashen faced.

"He fell down the stairs, his neck's broken. He's dead, Hilary," her voice rose to a shrill level as she looked down at the man's body, "we'll have the Authorities round. If they see the carpet they'll say it's my fault."

"Of course they will," replied Hilda brutally, "because it is. I told you about those stairs myself, but you just ignored me. Anyway, let's see what we can do. Where are you thinking of putting him?"

"Over the cliff, it'll look as if he fell over when he was out walking. I'll report him missing tomorrow."

"That's no good. You'll still have the Authorities around and they will take this place apart. Who knows he stays here?"

"You, me, and any of the other guests we've had. He hardly ever goes out, I think it was too far for him to walk to the village."

"I doubt the other guests will remember him. You don't exactly get people coming back year after year do you?"

Soundlessly Mrs Moffat shook her head.

"How does he pay his rent?"

"He has a standing order with the bank. He said it was easier than carrying cash. I cash the odd cheque for him when he needs ready money. Oh dear, I'll have to ring the bank in the morning and cancel the standing order."

"No. Leave it be. I know exactly where we can park him, and no-one will be any the wiser. If you've got your puff back, pick him up and we'll get this done while it's still dark. Where's the torch?"

Mrs Moffat obeyed like an automaton, delving into a drawer and producing a large black torch. Between them, the two women manhandled the remains down the short cliff path to the clump of gorse bushes hiding the entrance to Hilda's cave. It was a shame she had to reveal it, she thought, she could hardly use it as a safe haven now if she had to share it with the unfortunate Mr Lancaster, but it would make an excellent mausoleum.

Once having settled Mr Lancaster's body neatly at the back of the cave, Hilda took Mrs Moffat's arm and guided the older woman back up to the guesthouse. She sat her at the kitchen table and busied herself with the kettle.

Abigail Moffat still looked as if she had been kicked in the stomach by a large and unpredictable horse. Hilda piled two heaped teaspoonfuls of sugar into one cup, and set it down in front of her employer. She splashed extra milk into her own cup, and sat down opposite the other woman.

"Drink that, you need it for the shock," Hilda had subtly changed places with her boss, and was now the person in charge.

Obediently Mrs Moffat sipped at the tea. She looked like a woman whose spirit had been broken.

"Tomorrow you will have to find out where the nearest carpet fitter is and get that stair carpet replaced," Hilda ticked off points on her fingers as she pondered their quandary, "I will clear Mr Lancaster's room and get it ready to relet. You are absolutely sure no-one will miss him?"

Mrs Moffat shook her head. The colour was starting to return to her face, and she looked gratefully across the table into Hilda's eyes. She really didn't know what to do, but Hilary was proving to be a tower of strength. She hadn't made her ring the Police, she had even provided the ideal hiding place for the unfortunate Mr Lancaster.

"Do you think it will work, Hilary?" she asked, a trifle pathetically.

"Of course it will work, *I* am organising it" replied Hilda haughtily, "and my name is Hilda, not Hilary, I'd be obliged, *Abigail*," she stressed the woman's first name, "if you would refer to me by that name in future."

She smiled benignly at Abigail Moffat, who nonetheless felt a cold shiver run down her spine.

Chapter 9

They drove into Danemouth the following morning in Abigail's old red Micra. There was a carpet shop on the edge of the town. Hilda had persuaded Abigail, or to be more precise she had commanded her, to get the stair carpet sorted out today. As they parked, Hilda glanced across the road, the Danemouth Sewing and Knitting Centre shop caught her eye. Wonderful, two birds with one stone.

She marched Abigail into the carpet shop and guided her around the various giant rolls of carpet. Abigail dithered over a pale beige and lovat green pattern. Hilda moved her firmly along the store until they found a plain wine red carpet.

"This will look much classier, Abigail, and it won't show the dirt like that beige one. I think we will decide on this, don't you?"

Abigail nodded.

Hilda strolled around the back of the shop. There were off cuts of carpet and linoleum stored along the back wall. She had measured the entrance hall and the stairs, noting down the figures in her straggly handwriting. A roll of lino in a neat brown parquet design caught her eye. The price was marked down to quite a reasonable figure. Hilda checked the measurements printed on the price tag, it would easily be big enough for the lobby. Hilda had scrubbed the old lino until her arms ached, but it always looked dingy once the door was opened, this would be much more welcoming.

"Abigail, we'll have this too. It will make all the difference to the place. We also need the lounge carpet replacing, but maybe we will leave that until next month, when we have received Mr Lancaster's next rent."

Abigail made a choking noise in her throat which Hilda chose to accept as acquiescence.

An appointment was made for the following day, the man explaining that the original carpet would need to be removed before he arrived. Hilda sighed, and assured him the place would be ready. She was going to be busy.

Abigail was still moving in a trance like state. Hilda pursed her lips. She might have to remove her if she was going to be a danger to her own discovery. She hadn't killed anyone herself for well over a year now, would she still have the old skills? Abigail would of course be more use if she could keep her alive. Hilda couldn't drive, and having access to Danemouth without having to resort to public transport was a distinct bonus. She still had several hundred pounds secreted in one of the long chines leading down to the beach. At least she hoped it was. She had been tempted many times to make the trip into Danemouth to salvage her cash but a natural caution had restrained her.

"Let's go and look in the shop over the way," Hilda suggested, steering Abigail across the road.

Hilda knew exactly what she needed, a sponge bar, a punch to make her own punch cards, a wool winder, and some blank punch card and she rattled off the list to the assistant. While the girl was collecting the items, Hilda wandered round, seeing what else they had. Half a dozen back issues of machine knitting magazines, and some cones of yarn were added to her haul. She would make a woolly Mr Lancaster she decided, just like the little gentlemen she had had to leave behind in her old house. She carefully chose a beige yarn, the closest shade she could find to flesh, and went in search of fabric paint pens.

Abigail was looking at a sewing machine, she was fascinated by it. It was quite a complicated one, it used cassettes to embroider motifs automatically. One of the assistants had come across and was busy demonstrating what it could do.

Hilda sauntered over.

"Oh look, Hilary, er Hilda, Hilly," Abigail spluttered as she strove to remember Hilda's name, "isn't it wonderful, I've always wanted one of those. I've seen pictures of them, but I've never seen one working before now."

"We have just bought a carpet," replied Hilda, glancing at the price tag, "but you could always buy one like this next month Abigail, if we leave the Lounge carpet for another month."

Abigail watched the twin needles moving in unison as they embroidered a rose bud on the piece of fabric held in the assistant's expert hands.

"Is it hard to do?"

"If you can sew a straight seam, you can learn to do this. We also give a set of lessons with any purchase of one of these, and of course, if you did get into difficulties you could always come in and we'd try and help you."

Abigail glanced at Hilda, a look of greed and longing had replaced the vacant trance like stare. She looked back at the embroidery machine, her eyes hungry with desire.

"We'll get the lounge carpet shampooed I think, Hilary," she touched the embroidery machine gently, "can I leave a deposit do you think?"

Chapter 10

Hilda sat at one of the tables in the dining room and looked into the lobby with some satisfaction. In place of the scratched grubby lino, there was now an expanse of neat brown parquet tiles. Laminated of course, wood parquet would have been far too expensive, but it added a warmth to the entrance of the guest house, and, more to the point, it looked clean. She shifted slightly in her seat and looked at the stairs. They were beautifully covered in a rich wine red carpet instead of the scruffy, and dangerous, carpet runner which had been there. What a difference a few hundred pounds had made to the place. Together with Hilda's ministrations in the housekeeping area, Travellers' Rest presented a clean and tidy front to the world. Now all they needed were guests.

Abigail Moffat sat across the table from her, immersed in a brochure about sewing machines. Hilda felt they made a nicely matched pair, her passion was knitting, and Abigail's was sewing.

Since they had shared their night-time adventure disposing of Mr Lancaster's body, Abigail had become a little more forthcoming to Hilda about her history. She admitted that since the death of her husband just over three years ago, she had let the place go. She had only had intermittent help from the village, and the place had gradually sunk into a state of disrepair. Guests didn't tend to stay too long, and never ever returned for a second visit.

Hilda nodded. She could see how the place had spiralled out of control. Well, that was over now, she was here. Without really knowing how it had happened, Abigail had succumbed to Hilda's authority, and now Hilda was in total charge. Abigail could feel a power coming from the other woman, a malevolence which chilled her, but also thrilled her. Abigail had not had much excitement in her life.

"We can't live on Mr Lancaster's contributions," Hilda was thinking out loud, "we need to get this place running on viable lines. It can be done Abigail."

"Yes, Hilary, that is I mean Hilda", agreed Abigail docilely.

Hilda frowned. Was the stupid woman ever going to get her name right? Then again, perhaps it had been a mistake to admit that her name was really Hilda. Suppose someone overheard, and had an inkling of who she really was? That name could seal their suspicions.

"Just call me Hilly," said Hilda, "Hilly, or Mrs Wolfe if there are others around. I will call you Mrs Moffat when we are not alone. Do you think you can do that?"

"Yes Hilly. I'm sorry, I keep thinking about, you know," she glanced towards the cliff top which held the cave where Mr Lancaster was hidden.

"Forget him," ordered Hilda. "Put him right out of your mind. Mr Lancaster has gone to live with the angels. Remember Abigail, any mistakes and it will mean prison, and you wouldn't like prison. I know, I've been there."

Again Abigail felt the malevolence. She realised with a jolt that this woman was really dangerous, and she had let herself be implicated with her. But no, that was not really fair. She had already been trying to get rid of the body when Hilda had appeared so opportunely. She knew in her heart of hearts that if she had managed to tumble old Mr Lancaster over the cliff, the Police would have soon back tracked to Travellers' Rest, and she doubted if she would have been able to successfully feign either ignorance or innocence of the old man's demise. So she must sup with the devil. She looked across the table as Hilda lifted her cup of tea to her lips and drank greedily, and it certainly was a devil she was supping with.

"Tell me about that couple," said Hilda suddenly.

"What couple, Hilly?"

"The rumpty pumpty one, you mentioned it when I first came. How did you know they weren't married?"

"It was just a feeling. They were skittish, giggly, and they weren't a young honeymoon couple they had a few years behind them. Nothing you could put your finger on. I know when Mr Moffat and me were that age we had finished with all that sort of nonsense." Her lips pursed into a thin line and she nodded sagely at Hilda.

"It's quiet here," mused Hilda, "we could advertise it as a quiet, secluded romantic getaway. Adults only, no children. They're not family sized rooms anyway." She jerked her head in the direction of the Guests' floor.

"We've had the odd child here before," pointed out Abigail, "they liven the place up."

"They also wander about the place, exploring. We don't want one of the little darlings finding the cave now, do we?"

Abigail blanched.

"I didn't think…."

"You don't have to, let me do the thinking," replied Hilda coldly.

"Adults only, we can advertise in some Singles magazines, perhaps even a Gay one."

Abigail opened her mouth to protest, Hilda quelled her with a look.

"And over sixties, you never know what we might end up with. Another Mr Lancaster perhaps."

"I'm not sure if I want another permanent guest," replied Abigail, "he could be a lot of trouble could Mr Lancaster when he was in one of his moods."

"They don't necessarily have to be permanent," Hilda looked Abigail squarely in the eyes, "if they are not likely to be missed, why go to the bother of keeping them. Once they've set up regular payments, of course."

"Do you mean…..?" Abigail sounded scared and elated both at the same time.

"It would be nice for Mr Lancaster to have a bit of company. He might be lonely where he is, even with the angels. We wouldn't want anybody with him who we didn't know or approve of, now would we?"

Abigail's stomach did a flip, but there was something, a feeling she couldn't identify, a need that she had to satisfy. Could this be it? Perhaps she could make a suggestion, if she pleased Hilly she might let her help.

"What about the unmarried couples," asked Abigail, "well I reckon they are married, but not to each other if you know what I mean? Perhaps we could suss them out, then ask them for a little extra just so that their families don't get wind of what they are up to?"

Hilda stared at her, a look of shock had materialised on her face.

"Blackmail, Abigail? Oh no we couldn't do that, that's not nice, and anyway, it's illegal."

Abigail pointed towards the cliff.

"That's not legal either."

"That, Abigail, is business. If we were to try anything untoward with a family man, we would have the Police round our ears. Relatives get nosey, we need people without ties. Be guided by me, I have experience in this sort of thing. We will change Travellers' Rest into a love nest for those with loose morals, and anything that falls into our laps which won't be claimed we will deal with. Still, at least you are thinking now Abigail, if you get any other ideas, run them past me. We could have a good partnership here, you and me."

Chapter 11

Hilda Hopkins dropped the teabag into the kitchen bin and added milk to her cup.

"I'll be up in my room, Abigail. I want to get the back of that cardigan finished, the one I'm making for you with the pansy panels down the front. Once I've finished on the machine I'll bring it down to do the Swiss darning while we are watching the telly. A bit of extra colour in the middle of the flower heads will really bring it to life."

"All right. I'm just going to sort out these brochures, and get rid of the old ones, then I'll make a coffee and join you in the Lounge."

The two women had got into the habit of using the Guests' Lounge when they had no-one staying at the guest house. The sofa and armchairs were comfortable, and there was a large screen television installed in there. All Hilda had in her room was a small portable black and white set. Abigail had a colour television in her sitting room, but she liked to keep the room private to herself. So they compromised and took advantage of the place when they were alone.

Abigail wasn't expecting any guests until much later today. The weather outlook wasn't encouraging, the sky was already grey and overcast, and rain was forecast. She hummed quietly to herself. She was looking forward to seeing how Hilly was getting on with her new cardigan. Abigail loved to sew, and at Hilda's instigation she had made most of the soft furnishings in the guest bedrooms, turning one of the doubles into a frilly pink love nest, and the other into a starker, more masculine room. Hilda had decided to plumb the market for discreet venues for couples, mostly unwed, at least to each other, and provide a safe, no questions asked setting for the odd spot of naughtiness.

The two singles had been left as ordinary run of the mill hotel bedrooms. Clean, neat, but nothing spectacular for a bed and breakfast establishment. Hilda had explained to Abigail that they needed to cater for all tastes, and needs.

They had had several couples staying with them in response to a judiciously worded advertisement in a Singles magazine, and a similarly phrased classified ad in a Gay magazine had also produced good results. There had been some odd sounds emanating from the rooms now and again, but the two ladies tactfully forbore to comment, and three of the couples were now returning on a regular basis. A new couple were booked in for this evening. It was a Mr and Mrs Smith, it usually was, Abigail found her guests very unimaginative when it came to aliases, but they weren't due until after seven o'clock that evening. Abigail understood that they were coming from the London area, and, for whatever reason, they wouldn't be able to set out until late afternoon. Their room was all ready, fresh linen on the bed, fresh flowers on the dressing table, so Abigail felt that she and Hilly were entitled to their quiet afternoon in.

She could hear the whoosh, whoosh as Hilly moved the carriage backwards and forwards across the needle bed of her knitting machine. Hilly was so clever with her knitting. She had made several attractive twinsets for herself and for Abigail, and her latest creation for her partner was a long line cardigan, with a panel of pansies down each front. It would be pretty and colourful, Abigail had already seen the pieces which Hilly had completed.

There was a knock at the front door. Abigail looked up, surprised. They didn't often get passing trade here. She slipped the chain on the catch and cautiously opened the door.

A middle aged woman was leaning against the door jamb, one foot turned to one side.

"Oh good afternoon. I wonder, do you have any vacancies, I've hurt my foot and I'd really like to have a night in to rest it."

Abigail slipped the chain and invited the woman to enter. She was dressed in an anorak and trousers, and had a stout pair of walking boots on her feet. Abigail retreated around the Reception counter.

"These boots are still fairly new. I thought I'd walked them in, but I've a terrific blister on my heel. It feels like it's the size of a duck egg, and I don't want to walk any farther on it. It's too painful."

"Oh dear," twittered Abigail, "I'm sorry to hear that er Mrs er…?"

"Pritchard, Joyce, Miss," the reply came out staccato fashion. "I've got some gel plasters in my first aid kit, but it's at the bottom of my bag. First thing I thought to put in, I didn't think I'd have to empty the lot out to use it!"

She gave a deep baying laugh.

Abigail managed to produce a weak smile.

"We have a single bedroom available," she said, "it's £25 for one night, and you'll get a breakfast in the morning."

Joyce Pritchard nodded. She had taken a mobile phone out of her pocket and was squinting at the screen.

"I can't get a signal. I wanted to let my friend know I'd decided to deviate off the paths of righteousness."

Again there was the deep baying laugh.

Abigail gave her another uncertain smile, she didn't really understand the allusion the woman was making.

"I'm afraid those things don't work here, you have to go down the coast road almost to the village, and unfortunately we're waiting for the engineer because our landline is having problems."

This wasn't true, but Hilly had insisted that Abigail should never allow a guest to use the guest house phone, and the "Engineer on his way" excuse was the usual one.

"Oh well, doubt I'll be missed, there's nobody waiting for me at home, I'm my own woman."

Abigail felt herself flinch as the laugh boomed out again.

Joyce placed her rucksack on the counter and started digging through it explaining that she kept her wallet near the bottom to deter pick pockets.

'Chance would be a fine thing,' thought Abigail as the counter rapidly disappeared under a pile of belongings.

"Here we are." Joyce Pritchard fished a bulging wallet out of the bag and rummaged through it. Two ten pound notes and a five pound one fluttered onto the counter. Abigail couldn't take her eyes off the wallet in Joyce's hands, it was crammed with banknotes.

"If you'd like to go through to the Lounge I'll bring a basin of warm water and you can see to your foot," suggested Abigail, "get it sorted and a plaster on it before you tackle the stairs?"

"Excellent idea, I'll leave the bag here until I'm ready to go up." It was a statement rather than a request. Abigail nodded and turned to go into the kitchen. Her stomach was churning, all that money, and no-one knew she was here. She would deal with the woman all by herself. That would show Hilly that she was capable of doing "the business" as Hilly called it, without any help. Hilly got a bit overbearing sometimes; this would take her down a peg or two. Abigail's mouth felt dry. She reached across to the back of the work unit. They usually had a bottle of red wine on the go, and there was one there now. She took a quick swig, Dutch courage she thought. She quickly filled a plastic bowl with warm water and carried it through to the Lounge. Joyce had removed her boot and sock, and was contemplating a large angry looking blister on her heel.

"Not quite duck egg sized," she said ruefully, "but it certainly feels like it. Thanks very much."

She gingerly placed her foot in the bowl, wincing as she did so.

Abigail scurried across to the kitchen. What could she use? She was completely unaware of the fact that Hilda always sedated her victims before despatching them. She looked hastily around the kitchen. Near the back door was a short length of plastic clothes line. Hilda had put a new line up several days earlier, and this piece had been left over. Abigail picked it up, it was just over three foot long. It would do, it would go round the woman's neck.

She sidled into the Lounge and stood behind the settee.

"Is that better?"

"Much, thank you."

Abigail took a deep breath before snapping the clothes line around the rambler's neck.

"I'm sorry. I've got to," she squealed, hauling on the ends of the washing line.

Joyce Pritchard's hands had shot up to her throat, trying to tear the constriction away from her neck. The washing line was plastic coated, and Abigail felt it slipping between her fingers. Joyce Pritchard had kicked over the basin of water, her booted foot kicked the coffee table across the room. Abigail was shouting at her to stop fighting, to just let go.

There was a pounding on the stairs as Hilda came rushing down to investigate the noise. She took in the situation at a glance. Snatching up a cushion from where it had fallen on the floor, she pressed it over Joyce's face, bearing down with all her weight on the other woman until she felt her go limp.

Hilda removed the cushion, and deftly pulled on the clothes line to tighten it around the woman's neck, twisting it round and round so that it wouldn't unwind.

"Who the hell is she?" asked Hilda, "What have you done Abigail?"

"She's got loads of money, Hilly, and no-one knows she is here, and I wanted to show you I could do something all by myself."

Hilda gazed at her. She closed her eyes momentarily and bit back the retort which had sprung to her lips.

"She's only wearing one shoe," Hilda looked at the body.

"Her foot hurt, she was bathing it," Abigail replied in a small voice. Was Hilly cross with her? She hoped not, she had done this for both of them.

Hilda had found the discarded shoe and sock and was busy pulling them onto the woman's bare foot.

"What..." began Abigail.

"We have to make sure there is no evidence lying around. For goodness sake get some towels and the mop and clear that water up. We've got guests coming tonight remember."

Hilda looked at Joyce Pritchard's body, it would have to stay here for the time being, it was too light for them to risk crossing the headland with it and carting it down the cliff path to the cave. She hauled the body off the settee and by dint of much pulling and pushing secreted it between the sofa and the wall.

Abigail was busy mopping up the water while Hilda put the coffee table to rights and returned the cushions to their proper place.

It was done, the place looked pristine again, apart from the dead body behind the sofa and a damp patch on the hearth rug of course. Hilda sat down and inspected the room with a keen eye. It looked all right, they just needed to keep the Lounge door closed and direct their guests up to the bedroom.

Abigail took the mop away, and returned holding Joyce Pritchard's wallet and rucksack.

"Look," she tentatively offered the wallet to Hilda, "There really is a lot of money in here, Hilly."

"Just make some tea," Hilda replied, ignoring the proffered wallet, "I'll be through once I've got rid of the rucksack."

She sat looking at the thing. She would put it in the cave, it was too dangerous to leave it around here. She felt tired, but it had better be done now. She hauled herself to her feet and headed for the small path at the top of the cliff. She glanced at the notice that now adorned the start of the pathway. "Dangerous path, no entry" it really looked quite official. Hilda had produced it, and was quite proud of the effect. She hoped it would serve as a deterrent to anyone who wanted to stroll down the cliff path to the cove below.

Joyce Pritchard's body still lay behind the sofa in the Lounge, they would have to wait until the early hours before they could dispose of that. And there were guests due this evening too, another Mr and Mrs Smith.

Chapter 12

"Norman, there's a pair of boots sticking out from behind the sofa."

The young red haired woman had opened the Lounge door, and was looking into the room.

Hilda smiled, and moved deftly around the Reception counter.

"That's quite alright, Miss er, Mrs Smith," it was always Smith wasn't it, she reflected sourly, "That'll be Mrs Moffat having her afternoon nap. She's a little eccentric."

She thrust a key into the girl's hand while firmly shutting the Lounge door.

"You'll be wanting to see your room after your long journey I'm sure. Get yourselves settled. You're in the Pink Room, top of the stairs, on the left. I'll get Mrs Moffat up then I'll bring some tea into the Lounge for you, and a plate of sandwiches. Unless you'd prefer coffee?"

"Come along Sharon," urged Norman Smith, "let's have a look at this room. And yes, I would prefer coffee please, and so would Sharon."

Sharon opened her mouth as if to refute this, but catching a warning look in Norman's eye, muttered that coffee would be fine.

Hilda followed them halfway up the stairs and was in time to hear Norman ask Sharon what was she thinking of, drawing attention to herself in that way. Discretion, that was the key, did she not understand?

The reply was lost as the bedroom door closed, but Hilda smiled to herself as she returned to the ground floor. Norman Smith or whoever he really was didn't want any attention drawn to the fact that he was here with "Mrs Smith", a girl who looked better suited to be passed off as his daughter rather than his wife.

Abigail was hovering just inside the kitchen. Hilda hissed at her to come quickly. Together they lifted Miss Pritchard's dead body, and scurried across the lobby to Abigail's sitting room where it was dumped unceremoniously behind the bay window curtains, out of sight to a casual glance. Hilda snatched up a couple of cushions off Abigail's settee and pushed the other woman out of her room and back across to the Lounge. Hilda dropped the cushions behind the settee and told Abigail to lie down and feign sleep, but to make sure her feet were sticking out at the end of the sofa. Abigail complied. She had learnt it was easier to do as Hilly suggested, she didn't have to think, Hilly would make it all right.

Hilda hurried back into the kitchen and plugged in the kettle. She buttered some bread, and laid slices of ham between them, cutting them into dainty triangles as she had seen Abigail do. Hilda's usual attempts at ham sandwiches for her own consumption could more closely be described as doorsteps. Finally the coffee was made, well laced with valerian, she needed the pair to sleep soundly tonight while she and Abigail transported Miss Pritchard down to the cave in the cliff.

She had just carried the tray through when she heard a step on the stairs. Sharon was looking down, a little doubtfully. Hilda plastered a welcoming smile on her face, not an easy task considering her natural disadvantages, and brightly assured Sharon that supper was ready. Was Mr Smith not coming down?

"He'll be down in a sec," replied Sharon. She had descended the stairs, but was hovering uncertainly by the Lounge door.

"Oh silly me," chirped Hilda, "I've left Mrs Moffat behind the sofa. You have to excuse her dear, it's a hangover from the war, she was only a child you know when the family were blitzed out."

Sharon was impressed. The war was something she had heard about in History classes at the comprehensive school she had attended, and she had seen several war films on the television, but she hadn't realised there were still people around who actually remembered it. How strange. Norman came clattering down the stairs and took Sharon by the elbow.

"Come along, I'm famished. You're not still frightened about your body are you?" he laughed.

Hilda pushed into the Lounge ahead of them and approached the back of the settee.

"Mrs Moffat, ma'am, we have guests. You'll have to get up dear."

Abigail sat up, and wished the two strangers a good evening. She climbed to her feet, asked if that was the time, hoped they would enjoy their supper, and shuffled out of the room.

Norman and Sharon exchanged baffled glances.

"There you are, she's fine now she's had her little nap." Hilda pointed to a small hand bell on the mantelpiece. "Just ring if you want anything else. We have some nice carrot cake in the kitchen this evening."

She closed the door and leant against it for a moment, letting her breath out in a long, deep sigh. She could hear Sharon's shrill tones through the panels.

"It had different shoes, the one I saw, Norm, it was wearing hiking boots, not slippers."

"Eat up, Sharon, we can't make a fuss. You know what's at stake. There would be hell to pay if Felicity ever got wind of this. You're probably mistaken anyway, those two old ladies are hardly likely to be hiding dead bodies in a guest house lounge now are they?"

"I'm sorry Norman. I'm just so nervous. I've never done this before."

"Tell you what poppet, once we're well away from here tomorrow, we'll ring the Police anonymously, get them to have a snoop round. Does that make you feel any better?"

Hilda pursed her lips. Norman had just signed his death warrant, and the girl's too. Time for a cup of tea, she and Abigail were going to have a busy night.

When she returned to the kitchen Abigail had already made the tea. Hilda sat down and picked up her cup.

"We have another problem, Abigail. Mr and Mrs Smith intend being upstanding citizens tomorrow and setting the Police on this place."

Abigail paled.

"What are we going to do?"

"Guess," replied Hilda laconically, "once the valerian takes hold, we'll get rid of them. That's three we'll need to park in the cave tonight. We are going to be busy."

"Can we manage all that?" asked Abigail, doubtfully.

"Of course we can," snapped Hilda, "it's just a matter of timing and management."

And she managed it, very nicely too, despatching Norman first, then smothering Sharon as she dozed on the Lounge sofa. She had taken the car keys out of Norman Smith, or rather, as she found when she emptied his wallet, Norman Miller's jacket pocket, and told Abigail to move the car round to the back of the guest house.

"Tomorrow you can drive it into Danemouth, and get the train back. Leave it in a back street or something, not anywhere where it's likely to get a ticket. It'll be a while until it's missed. And wear gloves all the time you are driving it, do you understand?"

Abigail nodded.

"Good, that's sorted," sighed Hilda, "but for goodness sake Abigail don't do anything like that again on your own. Look at the trouble you've caused. Three in one night, that's got to be a record, even for me."

"I'm sorry Hilly," said Abigail apologetically, "I just wanted to see if I could manage it all by myself."

"You know now that you can't," replied Hilda bluntly. "We need to sort out what to say if the Police come looking for the Pritchard woman, they're not likely to expect the Smiths to have been staying here."

Abigail paled.

"I didn't think about that. Shall I say she might have fallen over the cliff, off the path?"

"Don't be completely silly," snapped Hilda, "don't you dare draw anyone's attention to that path. We don't want the Police poking around down there. Suppose they find the cave?"

Abigail looked crestfallen.

"I'm not clever about these things, Hilly, I don't know what to do."

"It's very simple. You just deny ever having seeing her. She either didn't get this far, or she must have continued towards the village unobserved. Don't mention the path. Do you think you can manage that? Remember this one wasn't manslaughter, this one was murder, that's life in prison Abigail, and at our age that would be life."

Chapter 13

As it happened Abigail wasn't called upon to try and dupe the Police.

Which was as well, Hilda thought afterwards, because she would never have managed it. Abigail had gone off to the Cash and Carry at Danemouth, leaving Hilda to man the fort. Hilda's heart had shot into her mouth when she saw the Police patrol car draw up outside the guest house. She took a deep breath, and when the bell rang, she opened the door with a welcoming smile on her face.

"Oh, good afternoon. I thought you were guests. Can I help?", Hilda had the confusion off to a nicety. She recognised neither of these men from her unwitting visit to Danemouth Police Station a year or two back, and they obviously had no idea who she was. No idea at all......

"We are looking for a Miss Pritchard, she's a rambler who has been reported missing. She set out a few days ago to do the coastal walk, and didn't check back with her friend when she was supposed to. We wondered if you had seen anything of her Mrs...?"

"Moffat" replied Hilda firmly, "Abigail Moffat. We don't have anyone staying at the moment." She smiled, "I was hoping when you rang the bell that you were passing trade."

"And you've not seen any lone women walking past here?"

"I'm afraid not."

Hilda stepped back and opened the door wider,

"You're very welcome to come in and look around. We only have the four bedrooms, two doubles and two singles, and they are all vacant at the moment. It's the recession, we're desperate for company actually."

"We?" queried one of the constables.

'Damn it,' thought Hilda, 'he's quick off the mark.'

"I run the place along with my partner, Hilary Wolfe, she's gone off to the Cash and Carry. If you have a number I can ask her if she has seen any strangers about and give you a ring. I don't suppose 999 would be appropriate?"

"Indeed not," smiled the constable, "emergencies only that one. Here you are ma'am."

He handed over a small business card with the number of Danemouth Police station inscribed on it.

"Thank you for your time, Mrs Moffat. I don't see any need for us to disturb you further."

Hilda leant against the closed door for a long time after they had driven off. That had been a close shave, but she felt she had pulled it off very smoothly.

Abigail found Hilda in the kitchen when she arrived home from the Cash and Carry, sipping at a cup of tea, Hilda's elixir for all troubles. Hilda told Abigail about the visit from the Police. Abigail sat down with a thump.

"Oh thank goodness it was you, Hilly," she twittered, "I would have gone all to pieces."

'Yes, you would', thought Hilda. Aloud she commented,

"We might have to keep up this pretence of identity. Just in case the Police do come back. Have you been to the dentist recently Abigail?"

Abigail was thrown by the change of subject.

"Dentist?"

"Yes a dentist," snapped Hilda impatiently, "to have your teeth seen to?"

"Not for years, decades, must be at least twenty if not more."

"Me too, so we are not likely to have any records anywhere handy. We'll book into a dentist in Danemouth. You will go as me and I will call myself Abigail Moffat. Do you have a bus pass?"

"I'm entitled, but I never bothered claiming it. I always drive myself in the car, and the bus service round here is rubbish as you know." Abigail sounded completely confused.

"Right then, I'll get a bus pass with my picture and your name. Don't worry Abigail, you'll still have your own identity for when you need it, you've got your driving licence and birth certificate haven't you?"

"But why do you need my bus pass and why should we swap identities at the dentist?"

"It's just insurance Abby, if we need to confuse the police. They could be chasing me, as one Abigail Moffat, while you will have the chance to get away safely. You will be able to prove you are you, but I won't. You will be quite safe."

Abigail didn't quite follow the reasoning behind this, but as usual, she fell in with Hilda's wishes, and a week later Hilda found herself in possession of a second identity, or indeed a third one, from Hopkins to Wolfe to Moffat. The visit to the dentist had been unpleasant. Hilda had had to have two fillings, and she hated the scraping when her teeth were cleaned, but it was all in a good cause, and Abigail had suffered more, she had had to have a tooth extracted! They had each promised faithfully to return in six months time, but both women knew they had no intention of ever going back. Hilda grinned, she would have to concentrate on who exactly she was supposed to be!

Under Hilda's tutelage, Abigail Moffat had rung Danemouth Police Station, given her name as Hilary Wolfe, and had earnestly assured the police sergeant that no pack backers had passed her house. This of course was perfectly true. Joyce Pritchard had not passed the house, she had been killed inside it.

Chapter 14

"We have to go to the Church Fete on Saturday," said Abigail, "we've not got anybody booked until Monday, and that's another Mr and Mrs Smith."

Hilda was busy sewing up the sleeve seam on her latest jumper. She looked across the sitting room at her companion.

"The Church Fete? Why on earth should we go to that?"

"It's a bit of a surprise," Abigail glanced warily at Hilda, "there's a needlework competition Hilly, and I've put a couple of things in for it."

Abigail was an avid needle woman. She had purchased a state of the art embroidery machine, and under Hilda's guidance, she had made several cushions, curtains and bedding sets which had transformed the two double guest bedrooms. They now had the Pink Room, which was frilly and frothy, and the Blue Room, a much starker décor, more masculine.

"That's nice dear. I'm sure you will be in the running for a prize. You must have a look in the shop and see if they have any new patterns."

Hilda needed to keep Abigail firmly under her thumb, flattery and the promise of more luxuries would help she knew.

"I er put Mr Lancaster in as well. I didn't think anyone would know who he was supposed to be by now."

"What!" the retort shot out of Hilda's lips and she half rose in her chair. Abigail cringed back on the settee.

"Your little doll is so good Hilly, I felt sure you would win."

"Tell me what you have done Abigail. Slowly and in detail. You've put the doll in for the competition?"

Abigail nodded.

"Did you give them my name?"

"Not yet, I was a little flustered and the lady from the Committee thought I'd done the cushion and the doll so she put my name on both the entry forms, and I didn't like to point out that she had got it wrong."

Hilda sat back in her chair and closed her eyes.

"Why didn't you tell me? I wouldn't have let you take it."

"That's why, I wanted to surprise you, Hilly."

'Yes,' thought Hilda 'with a visit to the Police Station if anyone recognises my work. Don't fluster her, if she panics we will come unglued.'

"I do wish you had told me, Abby. It might not be such a good idea to have the doll on show you know. Suppose someone does recognise him, they might want to know where he is now. Never mind, it's done now. It might cause more questions if we try to retrieve him. If it does get a mention, Abby, I want you to pretend that you made him. Can you do that? As a favour to me? Please?"

Hilda creased her face into a semblance of a smile. It was supposed to be winsome, but only served to accentuate the cruel lines around her mouth. Abigail bit her lip.

"If that is what you want Hilly, of course I will. I'm sorry, have I done something wrong again? I only wanted to please you, to surprise you, I'm sure Mr Lancaster will win."

Hilda gazed at her horror stricken as another thought struck her.

"What did you describe it as? Did you mention Mr Lancaster at all?"

"Oh no, I said his name was Fred." Abigail looked at Hilda with a touch of asperity, "I'm not stupid Hilly."

"Of course not. Fred, I like that, it suits him. What was Mr Lancaster's first name?"

"Ralph."

"Oh well, it's done now, let's just see what Saturday brings. Hopefully it may be rained off."

Chapter 15

Saturday dawned bright and clear. By the time the fete started at 2pm the sky was a bright blue, and the sun shone warmly on the proceedings. The Guest House had been locked, there wasn't much chance of passing trade on a Saturday afternoon on the headland, and Abigail had driven the pair of them down to Grime's Cove.

They paid their 50 pence entry fees, collected a programme each and wandered into the Fete. Abigail tried her hand on the Tombola and came away beaming with delight having won a can of lemonade. Hilda forgo to point out to her that she could have bought three cans for the money she had spent on tickets. Keep Abigail content was the order of the day; she didn't need the woman in panic mode.

Hilda found two knitting books on the second hand book stall. They both dealt with hand knitting, but she was sure she could adapt the patterns for her knitting machine. She started to perk up, maybe this Fete was going to be fun after all.

They approached the marquee where the competition entries were housed, with some trepidation. There were several stalls in there. Apart from the needlework stall there had been a cake making competition, an art competition, and a garden produce competition. Hilda made straight for the needlework stall. Mr Lancaster, or "Fred" as Abigail had re-christened him was standing proudly in the centre of the stall, with a red rosette pinned to his chest. One of Abigail's cushions, a pretty heart shaped piece in pale pink silk, embroidered with tiny flowers which reflected the heart shape had a blue rosette attached to it.

"First place and second place," murmured Hilda, secretly thrilled that her knitted doll had done so well, "well done Abigail, your cushion looks lovely."

Abigail smiled. It was going to be all right. She rather wished that the placings had been reversed, hers first and Hilly's second, but Hilly was pleased, that was the most important thing. One of the committee ladies bore down on them. She completely ignored Hilda and spoke directly to Abigail.

"Hello again, Mrs Moffat, didn't you do well? The Judges' had a very difficult decision with your work, they are both so good. We decided to give you First on the doll it is so unique. There'll be a presentation at four o'clock, you'll be getting a little silver cup to keep as a memento. I do hope you'll still be here?"

"Oh, yes. Thank you," murmured Abigail faintly, with a worried glance at Hilda. "I think we'll go and have a cup of tea."

"They're doing cream teas in the Parish hall, homemade scones and real strawberry jam."

Four o'clock arrived. Abigail and Hilda retired to the competition tent. Hilda sat herself right at the back, urging Abigail to go and sit on a chair in the front row.

The prize giving took some time. First of all there were the awards for the children's Fancy Dress; this was followed by the vegetable competition. First prize went to the gardener from the local Manor House, a decision which caused much muttering and grumbling from the other competitors. The cake competition came next, followed by prizes in the painting section, and then it was the presentation for the needlework contest.

Abigail was called forward last, as the runners up were presented with their rosettes first. She approached the stall, blushing a deep crimson, and took the small cup from the judge's hands.

"Smile."

Abigail looked round in some confusion as a camera flashed.

"Can you just hold the doll next to the cup, please?"

Abigail clutched Fred in one hand, the cup in the other, and the camera flashed again.

"Lovely, just a couple of details, it's Abigail Moffat I know, saw it on your entry form, have you been crafting long?"

"About a year, recently, but most of my life I suppose, really, it's my hobby" twittered Abigail.

"Lovely, thank you very much. Don't forget to buy a copy of the Danemouth Gazette, you'll see your picture in there. Oh and congratulations on your win."

Abigail gave the young reporter a weak smile. What would Hilly say? Still, it was her picture in the paper, not Hilly's, and hopefully no-one would associate the unfortunate Mr Lancaster with "Fred".

Chapter 16

Mike Patterson glanced through a copy of the Danemouth Gazette. A picture caught his eye. It showed an elderly woman gleefully clutching a small silver cup, and holding a knitted doll in her arms. Sergeant Patterson had been on duty a couple of years or so ago when the Midchester Police had apprehended a female serial killer here in Danemouth. That woman had made knitted effigies of her victims. He looked closely at the picture; it was somewhat grainy so he couldn't make out the woman's features clearly.

Mike rooted about in his desk drawer for scissors and cut the article out of the paper. He stuck it in an envelope and addressed it to DS C Naylor at Midchester nick. It might be something, it might be nothing, they could decide.

Claire Naylor was very interested indeed when she saw the cutting. She remembered the dolls very clearly, but this woman didn't look much like the Hopkins woman at a casual glance.

Claire picked up the telephone and rang the Danemouth Gazette. She explained where she was phoning from, and asked for a copy of the photograph of the Needlework competition to be sent to her. It arrived later that day by courier, and Claire eagerly perused it.

The doll was very well made, very lifelike, but according to the blurb, the craftswoman was one Abigail Moffat, and the doll's name was "Fred". All the Hopkins' dolls had been formally designated Mr So-and-so. Hopkins could have changed her own name of course, in fact she must have done, she had disappeared so completely. Claire picked up a magnifying glass and held it over the face in the photograph.

"Elementary my dear Sergeant," quipped a voice.

Claire glanced up at Graham Perkins.

"Very droll Graham, look at this. Recognise anything?" She pushed the photograph across to him.

"Haven't seen her before... oh!" he looked intently at the image, "isn't that one of those dolls, the ones from Merrydown Crescent?"

"Can't be, ours are all in the basement, in evidence boxes. But it's a bit of a coincidence don't you think?"

"Abigail Moffat it says here. But she's a lot skinnier than Hopkins, and the face is different. Hopkins has a face like a slapped arse."

Claire grinned,

"Very apt, if somewhat non-pc" she commented, "and this one is older too, according to this."

She passed the newspaper cutting across for him to read.

"Although you know," she continued thoughtfully. "I don't suppose Hilda Hopkins has the monopoly on knitted dolls, there must be hundreds of thousands of knitters around the country, and they won't all just stick to making cardigans, it's just that this one is so distinctive. Can you check her out, do you think, discreetly?"

"Discretion is my middle name Sarge, I'll get straight onto it."

"And there was I thinking your middle name was Percy," grinned Claire. "I can't imagine she would have stuck so close to home. My idea is that she's working in an old folks Home in Scarborough or somewhere as a carer. I just dread to get a report saying that she has decimated all the inmates in some institution or other."

Graham glanced up as he spotted a figure passing the CID room door.

"Erm, back in a sec Sarge."

He hurried after a tall auburn haired police woman.

"Babs, have you got a minute?"

Barbara Grey paused.

"I just wondered if you fancied dinner tomorrow night, that's all? There's a rather nice restaurant I know, just off the canal?"

"I can't, it's my BSL class."

Graham looked mystified.

"British Sign Language," explained Barbara, "I'm doing a course. I thought it might come in useful. I'm doing it off my own bat, it's not an official one, and I'm finding it really interesting."

"Oh okay then." Graham looked crestfallen, it had taken him some time to pluck up the courage to ask Barbara out.

"But I'm free on Thursday if the invite still stands?"

Graham returned to the CID room on cloud nine. He settled himself at his desk, and started to investigate Abigail Moffat.

It didn't take him very long. Records showed that Abigail Moffat had lived at Grimes Cove for well over fifteen years. She had been widowed some years ago, and now lived on her own in a small and apparently not overly successful guest house. Perkins found the details for her car, it had been MOT'd, was insured in her name and she had a valid driving licence. Further investigations showed that Council rates were paid regularly, and the woman had well established financial records, and held accounts at the local Cash and Carry warehouse. Whoever she was, she certainly was not Hilda Hopkins.

"It's not her, Sarge," he said, as Claire Naylor went past his desk. "Moffat must be into knitting too, unless Hopkins has been letting her enter competitions using her stuff, of course. But this one looks harmless enough."

He gazed at the slightly vacuous looking woman grinning sheepishly at the photographer, a small silver cup clutched in one hand, and a knitted doll held in the other.

"Hardly likely I agree," replied Claire, she read through the blurb attached to the photograph, "Apparently she got second prize for a cushion she'd made as well, something she had sewn and embroidered. Hopkins wasn't into that, she didn't have a sewing machine at her place so far as I remember, it was all knitting with her. And anyway Hopkins is too egotistical to let anyone else take the credit for any of her achievements. Do you remember her in Court? She was determined no-one else would be implicated, she absolutely revelled in what she had done. Thanks anyway Graham, it was worth pursuing. At least we know now she's not running a bed and breakfast within fifty odd miles of us!"

Chapter 17

"Hilly, I've made drop scones."

Abigail stood at the foot of the stairs, gazing up towards Hilda's bedroom.

"I'll be down in a moment," replied Hilda, "I just want to take this neckband off the machine."

"I've put the tray in the Lounge, may as well watch the big telly while we haven't got anyone in."

Hilda picked up a box of pins, threaded a tapestry needle through the front of her cardigan, and carried her knitting downstairs.

She settled on the sofa, and put her work down next to her. Abigail had gone back into the kitchen looking for a pot of jam, so Hilda busied herself pouring a cup of tea. Abigail's coffee was already made. Hilda wrinkled her nose, she didn't drink coffee herself, and she didn't much like the aroma of it either. Outside darkness had fallen early, and rain lashed against the windows of the Lounge. Hilda raised her tea to her lips and took a sip, this was grand, she was warm and comfortable, sheltered from the bad weather, and indulging in her passion for machine knitting. She lifted the jumper she was making onto her lap and deftly pinned the neckband into shape. She took the needle, threaded it with yarn, and began to neatly back stitch the neckband into place. Abigail bustled in and started spreading jam on the drop scones.

Hilda took a plateful and bit into one of them. It really was delicious, light and golden, topped with homemade strawberry jam. Abigail was a good cook, true it was plain British cooking, all the old favourites, nothing fancy, but it always tasted delicious. Hilda conceded that Abigail could please the patrons when it came to a full English breakfast, but she felt she was much better at more exotic fare. She often made a curry out of the left over meat. Abigail would gasp and drink copious glasses of water, but then, thought Hilda scornfully, she needed a bit of spice in her life. Hilda yawned, this was definitely the cat's whiskers. All they needed were a few more guests, just to keep the books in the black. Of course they had Mr Lancaster's contributions going into the bank regularly each month but business was still somewhat slow. There had been no response to their advert for long term elderly guests. Hilda was disappointed, she had thought a quiet retirement to the seaside would have suited a lot of people. A heavy gust of wind buffeted against the side of the house. Perhaps it was just a bit too bracing around here. Still, she reflected, they were starting to get a lot more couples looking for a quiet, discreet venue for their own nefarious purposes.

The front door knocker hammered against the wood. Hilda jumped, nearly spilling her tea.

"I'll go," she said, hastily replacing the cup on the coffee table.

There were two people standing on the doorstep, both absolutely soaked. As soon as the door opened the man pushed inside, shoving roughly past Hilda to get into the dry lobby.

"Come along Alice," he called, "get in before you get any wetter."

Hilda didn't think that was possible, water simply streamed off the pair of them.

"The car's stopped about two hundred yards or so from here. We've run out of petrol. Got lost in all these damn back lanes and not a garage in sight. I'll ring the AA in the morning, do you have any rooms free?"

Abigail appeared at the Lounge door.

"Indeed we have. We charge on a nightly basis, and we are very discreet."

She gave him a knowing smile.

The man frowned.

"My wife", he stressed the relationship, "and I are trying to get to Southhurst-on-Sea, we were booked on the cross channel ferry, but we got completely lost."

He scowled at his wife.

"My fault for letting her do the navigating of course. Now the damn car's packed up, and it's like a monsoon out there."

Hilda stepped forward holding out a large unfurled umbrella.

"If you want to grab your bag, Mr err? I'll put some towels in your room so you can get dry. We don't usually do evening meals but I'm sure we could rustle up a bowl of soup and some sandwiches?" She jerked her head at Abigail, directing her to the kitchen.

The man looked around the lobby with an expression of distaste on his features.

"Rooms by the night?"

His voice was full of innuendo.

Hilda realised that this pair were actually married to each other, and were not looking for a romantic interlude.

"We get a lot of passing trade," murmured Hilda, "it's a popular venue in the summer, lots of walkers use the coastal path. It's quite pretty when the sun is shining. So we accommodate from a night to a fortnight, whatever our guests prefer, Mr err?"

"Bryant," snapped the man, taking the umbrella from Hilda. "I'll fetch the bag."

"You come up with me, Mrs Bryant," said Hilda, "I'll show you the Pink Room while your husband gets your luggage."

She took the key and ascended the stairs, with Mrs Bryant dripping miserably behind her.

Hilda threw open the door of the Pink Room. Mrs Bryant took in the frills and froths, the heart shaped pillows, the very pinkness of the room.

"Oh, it's very….. er… pretty."

Hilda was rummaging in the airing cupboard next to the bathroom. She emerged with fluffy clean towels and handed one to Mrs Bryant who accepted it gratefully and starting rubbing her hair dry.

Hilda returned to the lobby, hovering by the door until she heard Mr Bryant arrive. She opened the door and retrieved the umbrella. He didn't look any less wet for using it.

Again she ascended the stairs, Mr Bryant bumping a suitcase along in his wake. She opened the door of the Pink Room and stepped back to let Mr Bryant have the full effect.

"My god, Alice, it's like a bordello."

He looked at Hilda, letting his gaze travel up and down her body.

"What is this place?"

He nodded at the other bedroom door.

"What's that one like?"

Hilda scurried downstairs and retrieved the key to the Blue Room. She really wanted to show this man the door, but would he cause trouble for them if she did? She opened the door to the second double room and let the prudish Bryant precede her.

"This is better, a bit stark but I can't be doing with all that fuss and frivolity in that other room. We'll take this."

Alice Bryant was called peremptorily, and joined her husband in the doorway.

"The first room was very pretty, Andrew, very pink" she said.

"Don't be so naïve woman, I'm not sleeping in a room like that. I hope you will be able to give us some sort of discount seeing that we have arrived well after booking in time," he added, looking at Hilda, I wouldn't want to have to get in touch with the vice squad or anyone about what I think this place is really used for."

"Andrew!" Alice had flushed a deep red. She mouthed 'sorry' at Hilda behind Andrew's back.

"Only joking," replied the man, taking the towel off Alice and starting to towel his head dry.

'Oh no you are not,' thought Hilda grimly, 'I will indeed give you a discount.'

Chapter 18

Hilda placed the Bryants' suitcases in the boot of their car, and slammed down the lid. Abigail had filled the tank from a small jerry can. There wasn't an awful lot of petrol in there, but with any luck it would be enough to drive the car as far as Danemouth.

"Do you think you can drive it, Abigail?" she asked anxiously.

"I don't see why not," replied Abigail, "it's bigger than mine, that's all. I managed that one of Norman Smith's all right and that was a different make to mine too. They all work the same way, Hilly."

Abigail was rather pleased that she could do something that Hilly couldn't. Hilda strapped herself into the passenger seat.

"Come on then."

It took Abigail a little time to get used to the Bryant's BMW, but by the time they arrived at the outskirts of Danemouth she was handling it as if she had driven it for years.

Hilda directed Abigail to the Grand Hotel on the seafront. This was where she had stayed when she was here with the coach excursion, and she knew there was a large car park to the rear of the establishment. They parked the car in a far corner. Hopefully it would be several days before it was discovered.

Hilary steered Abigail along the front towards one of the chines, the long valleys, which ran down to the sea.

"You stay here, and if anyone comes along, stop them," ordered Hilda.

"How?" Abigail was starting to panic.

"It's very simple, you can do it, Abigail, honestly. Ask them the time, the way to the railway station. Ask them if they are here on holiday and are they enjoying it. Say anything, just give me five minutes on my own."

Hilda marched off purposefully down the path, leaving Abigail standing forlornly at the top. Hilda looked about her keenly. Yes, this was where she had buried the spade, she was sure. She scrambled up the bank and started to dig with her hands. Her fingers touched plastic and she pulled out the bag and the spade. Now, one lot was by the gorse bush, another near that outcrop, and the other must be about here. Hilda dug frantically, she couldn't find anything in the hole. Had it been found? Surely one of the police officers would have mentioned it? She tried again a few inches to the left. There was something there. Hilda scrabbled with her fingers and drew out a small plastic bag. It was stuffed with banknotes. Hilda had hidden three lots of money in this chine when she had been on the run before.

She quickly found the second bag but the third one eluded her. Angrily she banged the spade on the ground in frustration. Where the hell was it? She couldn't dig up the whole side of the valley. She had to be quick, goodness knew what Abigail was doing. She shouldn't have left her on her own. Hilda slid down the slope towards the rocky outcrop. She jabbed the spade into the soil. Several inches down she found the third plastic bag. She was nearly faint with relief. She hurled the child's spade towards a clump of gorse, and stuffed the three plastic bags into the carrier in which she had originally hidden the spade. She had done it.

She hurried back up the chine. Abigail was still standing where she had left her, peering around fearfully.

"No-one came, Hilly."

"Good. You're doing well Abigail. Let's go along to the pier. What time do the shows finish, do you know?"

"About ten, we're much too late for a show Hilly."

Hilda sighed. "We need to get a taxi home, unless you fancy walking? If we pick one up at the end of the pier, the driver will think we have been to a show."

Abigail bit her lip. Hilly was so clever. She wouldn't have thought of hiding in a crowd of theatre goers. It hadn't even occurred to her that they would need transport to get back to the Guest House. All she had been concerned with was getting rid of the Bryants' car. Again it had been Hilly who had thought to bring kitchen wet wipes along and had cleaned all the surfaces of the car, including the visor and the rear mirror - Hilly had said car thieves always missed those, and that's how they got caught, she had seen it on the telly.

Hilda was speaking. Abigail came out of her reverie.

"Sorry, Hilly, what was that?"

"I said," repeated Hilda petulantly, "that it is a shame I can't drive. It would have been much better if we had been able to bring both cars. Once we are settled again, you can take me out and show me the basics."

"I'll have to ring the insurance people, get you put on as a named driver Hilly. And you'll have to get a Provisional Licence, and do the theory test. You can't drive until you've passed that I don't think."

"I'm not thinking of taking any test," snapped Hilda, "I just want to be able to move the car around if we need to. You can teach me down on the field where they hold the car boot sale. No-one will bother us there."

Hilda had timed it nicely. They had arrived at the entrance to the pier just as the crowds of tourists were leaving. They waited in line for a taxi, two elderly ladies lost in a long line of people.

The next morning Hilda was up and about early. She rummaged through the larder looking for Abigail's stack of empty jam jars. Abigail kept a good supply of these, and every so often had a jam making session, blackberry jam in the autumn when the blackberry bushes were full of fruit, strawberry jam to use up the glut of berries from the market in the summer, and she also made a rather good lemon curd. Hilda took four one pound jars and packed the money in them that she had taken from the chine in Danemouth. She also added several hundred pounds which she had removed from Abigail's bank account, leaving just enough in the account to cover cash and carry purchases and household expenses.

Hilda had decided it would be much better to have the money to hand. True they weren't getting any interest, but then, if the bank account grew too large, maybe there would be interest of another kind. Hilda wanted Abigail's affairs to look much the same as they had over the past few years, despite the extra business they were getting these days. She carried the jam jars outside, and carefully buried them in the flower bed. Nothing much grew along here, other than tough grass and gorse, it was just too windy. Abigail had planted marigolds and lobelia, but they were stunted and very unhappy looking. Still, this made an excellent hidey hole, no-one would guess what was just under the surface.

Chapter 19

Hilda Hopkins was busy cleaning the Lounge windows. She had already done the outside earlier that morning, and now she was working on the inside. The glass shone. Hilda enjoyed house work; she loved to see the place gleaming, and took great pride in her work. The transformation of the guest house from a run down, grubby establishment into a smart squeaky clean business place had been entirely due to Hilda's efforts.

She watched incuriously as a silver car drew into the parking space in front of Travellers' Rest. It was similar to the one the Bryant's had driven, she thought. Same colour anyway, Hilda had no idea about different car makes. Mr Bryant had tried to throw his weight about, and had hinted that he would report the Guest House as being little more than a brothel. Unfortunately he hadn't known what he was up against. A bowl full of Abigail's tasty vegetable soup, ham sandwiches and large mugs of coffee, well laced with valerian, had seen the couple pass peacefully into a sleep from which they were not allowed to awaken. They had joined the rising toll of bodies in the cave in the cliff side. Abigail and Hilda had left the Bryants' car in a hotel car park, and Hilda had no idea if it had been discovered yet.

This car must belong to the couple who had booked in for a two night stay. A Mr Perkins and his partner, not very imaginative, still it made a change from Smith. The passenger door opened and a tall, auburn haired young woman stepped out. Hilda gasped. She knew that face. She was a police officer, and not only that, she was the same bitch who had caught Hilda as she had tried to flee from the Danemouth Machine Knitting Exhibition nearly four years ago. She recognised the man now too. He had walked round to the back of the car and was lifting the lid of the boot. She didn't know his name, but he had sat in on several of the interviews, sitting quietly in the background taking notes. Were they here for her? Or was it simply a coincidence? Were they just looking for a cosy weekend getaway?

As these thoughts went through Hilda's head, she had been automatically gathering all her cleaning paraphernalia together. She rushed through to the kitchen.

"Abigail, we have a problem."

Abigail started.

"Now don't panic, it can be easily resolved. Listen to me carefully. I will stay in your bedroom, out of sight, and you will see to the guests."

Abigail looked bewildered. Hilda realised she wasn't explaining this very well.

"You know I've told you I was once in prison?"

Abigail nodded, although from what she remembered Hilly hadn't been very forthcoming about why. Persecution had come into it, and a misunderstanding about some bank accounts, but it had all been very vague.

"This pair are from the Police, but I think they are just here on holiday. It's not surveillance, they wouldn't be so blatant. They certainly wouldn't have used that Constable Grey woman, so if we are careful, they will stay for their holiday and then they will go away again."

Abigail was looking worried. Hilda hurried to reassure her.

"It's just a matter of them not seeing me. While they are on the premises I will stay in your bedroom, you use mine. If they ask about you being here on your own, say you have a cleaner but she's away."

Hilda remembered Susan Morris and her cleaner, Mrs O'Grady. Mrs O'Grady had gone off to Herne Bay to visit her son and his family, leaving the coast clear for Hilda to squat in the Morris's bungalow for several days.

"Tell them I'm visiting family in Stoke-on-Trent but you expect me back at the end of the week."

The door knocker clattered against the wood panel.

Hilda retreated towards Abigail's bedroom, while Abigail went out into the lobby to welcome the couple.

Chapter 20

"They are doing a talk at Grime's Cove Library about the eighteenth and nineteenth century smuggling activity around here," said Graham Perkins reading a flyer, "it's being done by the local Historical Society. It sounds good," he added wistfully, glancing at Barbara.

"Go if you want to," she replied cheerfully, "I could do with washing my hair. In fact, I could give myself a pamper night, facial, body scrub the lot. We're here to enjoy ourselves Gray, but we don't have to do everything together!"

"I'll come straight back afterwards," he promised.

"Bring some fish and chips if the shop is still open. I don't really fancy ham sandwiches, and there's nothing much else on the menu tonight."

"Your wish is my command," he grinned.

Barbara laughed, but she secretly thought he was such a sweet guy. She was getting really fond of him, could this be the real thing?

Graham departed, and Barbara started her preparations for her evening in. She had a lovely spa set, a recent birthday present from the Barcrofts, and she intended to indulge in a spot of me time.

She undressed and ran the water in the bath, may as well fill that up before she started plastering mud packs on her face. The water ran tepid. Bother, she would have to go and ask the landlady to turn on the heating. Barbara slipped into a pair of jeans and pulled a tee shirt over her head. The best laid plans of mice and men she thought.....

She went downstairs to Reception. It was empty but she could hear someone moving around in the kitchen. She went through the dining room and popped her head round the kitchen door.

"Excuse me Mrs Moffat, I was wondering if there would be any chance of some hot water......"

Barbara tailed off as the woman at the stove turned to face her. She knew that face, even with the hair set differently, this woman's hair was done up in a neat French pleat, rather than a messy perm, but the sheep like face with the hard eyes.....

"You! I know you!" cried Barbara, stepping forward.

Hilda Hopkins snatched up a wine bottle which was lying close to her hand and smashed it across the side of Barbara's head. The police woman went down like a felled ox.

Hilda looked about her wildly, and reached for the nearest thing to hand, a tea towel. She wrapped it round Barbara's neck and pulled for all she was worth. There was a blast of cold air, and Abigail Moffat let herself in through the back door. She stopped abruptly as she witnessed the scene in front of her. The young guest who Hilly had recognised from her past was lying on the floor and Hilly was strangling her! But Barbara Grey had someone with her, and since the Bryants, Hilly had always said they must only do away with single guests.

Hilda looked up.

"She's dangerous, she recognised me."

She looked down at Barbara's face. It was suffused purple, and her tongue was protruding from her mouth.

"Let's get her out of here. Never mind wrapping her up, just grab hold and let's get her down to the cave."

It was something of a struggle. Barbara was sturdier than most of the other victims, and it took the women some time to get down the path. Abigail suggested just dropping her over the edge.

"I've told you before, that is not only a stupid idea, it's risky. The Police would search all down here. Do you want to get caught?"

Abigail had shaken her head, crestfallen.

"Sorry Hilly, I didn't think."

'No' thought Hilda, 'you don't think do you my dear. I'm afraid our partnership is going to have to come to an end. You are just too dangerous to keep around.'

Barbara was dumped unceremoniously into the cave, just dropped on top of the pile of bodies like a sack of coal.

Back in the kitchen, Abigail sat at the table. Panic was starting to set in now that the action was over.

"Her young man went down to the library, there's a talk on he wanted to go to, I heard him telling her, but it'll be over by ten I bet. He'll want to know where she is. What are we going to say?"

"We'll tell him she had a phone call, rang for a taxi and left. Tell him she said she'll ring him in the morning. I'll sort out her stuff. Meanwhile Abby, you just sit there and relax and I'll make you a nice cup of coffee. I need a tea too before I get started."

Abigail smiled gratefully at Hilda.

"Oh Hilly, you are clever, you always know just what to do. I couldn't manage it."

"You don't have to dear." Hilda was busy crushing valerian tablets in with the coffee grounds, "not while I am here to look after you. Nothing can go wrong."

Abigail obediently drank the coffee which Hilda had made, and at her instigation, followed Hilda upstairs to the guest room.

"I need a second pair of eyes to make sure nothing is missed," explained Hilda, although she could see that Abigail's eyes were starting to look heavy with sleep.

"Of course," twittered Abigail, "I'll do my best Hilly. I just feel so tired."

Hilda looked at her, feigning a look of deep concern.

"Oh Abigail, how selfish of me. You helped to carry that girl all the way to the cave, and I forget sometimes that you are older than me, you just don't look it, that's the trouble."

Abigail blushed at the compliment.

"Now you come with me, we'll go up to my room, it's nearest, and you lie on my bed for half an hour. I'll see to all this. Half an hour's rest and you will be well able to cope with the messages when Mr Perkins comes back in."

Abigail allowed herself to be led upstairs. She lay on the bed and Hilda deftly removed her shoes. She picked up a pillow. Abigail flinched, but Hilda gently lifted her head and popped the pillow beneath it.

"There you are dear, that will be much more relaxing. You rest now."

Abigail was drifting off to sleep. How awful, for a moment she had thought dear Hilly was going to smother her with the pillow, but the sweet woman was just making sure she was comfortable. What a pig she was to harbour such thoughts about dearest Hilly. Her eyes closed and she sank into a deep sleep.

Hilda stood and looked down at the sleeping woman. It was a shame, Abigail had been the closest to a friend and confidante that Hilda had ever had. But she was a loose cannon. Better get rid of her now before she exposed the pair of them. She left the room, locking the door behind her.

Hilda stuffed Barbara's belongings in her suitcase and shoved it onto the back seat of the Micra. Gingerly she sat in the driving seat and started the engine. She had never really got the hang of driving despite all Abigail's patient tuition, she felt she just wasn't cut out to be a driver. Still, she could move the car as far as it needed to go, or almost, she didn't intend being with it on its final journey. She drove very slowly a little way down the headland until she came to the bend in the coast road. She got out of the car, released the brake, leaned into the driver's side and steered it towards the edge. The slope of the land and the car's own momentum did the rest, and it flew over the edge like an ungainly red bird. Hilda heard the crash as it landed far below and peered over the edge.

It was too dark to see much. She had hoped it would burst into flames, they always did in films, but there was no tell tale glow. Oh well, at least it was done, it would look as if Abigail had tried to flee with Barbara's luggage and had careered over the edge in her panic.

The young man Perkins would be back soon. She had to be gone before he arrived. Would he stay behind for a drink in the village pub, or would love's young dream be keen to return to his paramour? Hilda's lip curled.

She dug up the jars in the flower bed and tipped the money into her rucksack. Hilda had dressed in jeans, jumper and an anorak, with a pair of stout walking boots on her feet. She would pass herself off as a rambler. She went through Abigail's desk and the drawers in Reception, hunting for any spare cash and documents. She looked around the lobby. This had been a good place to stay. And she would have to leave her knitting machine and all her books and equipment behind. That was the biggest wrench. One more thing, then she could go.

Hilda took the matches off the kitchen shelf and went up to the guests' bedrooms where she ignited each bed. She hurried down stairs to the Lounge. Carefully she lit another match, and held it to the long curtains until the flames began to lick hungrily up the fabric. She scuttled into the dining room, pulled out the table cloths and set fire to them, before retreating into the lobby where she held a match to the rack of brochures. She went out through the front door, leaving it open to let a draught of air blow through the house.

Hilda lifted her rucksack onto her shoulders. There wasn't that much in it, apart from several thousands pounds, just a clean top, and two changes of underwear. She would be able to buy whatever she wanted anyway. Hilda glanced back at the Guest House, the flames had started to take a firm hold on the ground floor. Abigail wouldn't suffer, if the tablets didn't keep her sedated, the smoke would surely kill her long before the flames reached the top of the house.

Hilda resolutely turned her back on her old life and set out for the village. What a good job it was downhill all the way to Grime's Cove, she would be able to make good headway.

Hilda glanced at the Library as she passed by on the other side of the road. The lights were on and she could see Graham Perkin's silver car still parked in the car park. The talk must have gone on for longer than expected. All those enthusiasts, they were probably having an impromptu extension and chatting amongst themselves. Hilda let herself through the wicket gate at Grime's Grove Halt and crossed the bridge to the London side. There was a train to London in twenty minutes. Just before it arrived, a crowd of ramblers appeared, chattering and jostling amongst themselves. Hilda quietly attached herself to them and climbed onto the train as if she was part of the group. The doors slammed, and the train moved off.

Chapter 21

Barbara Grey's eyes fluttered and she restlessly moved her head from side to side. She was lying on her back. Her head throbbed, and her throat was sore. Something was sticking into her shoulders, something sharp, but also squishy. How was that possible? There was a smell too, a dreadful smell, just on the edge of her consciousness. She had smelt it before, but where, and when? She wriggled, trying to find a comfortable position. The floor was lumpy. Had she fallen out of bed? She opened her eyes. Everything was black. Dear god, was she blind? She sat up sharply. A wave of nausea passed over her, and she turned to one side and vomited. Her throat was on fire. The spasm passed, but now there were two appalling smells competing around her.

Barbara raised her head, more gently this time. Ahead of her she could see a slight difference in the blackness, a touch of grey, mottled grey but a lightness none the less. Would she be able to differentiate shades of grey and black if she was blind? Probably not. A wave of relief flooded through her. She crept slowly towards the patch of grey. What was she moving over, plastic by the feel of it, had someone stored their garbage in here? It would go some way to accounting for the stench.

She was crawling on her hands and knees. Could she stand, or would she get dizzy and fall? What was this place, some sort of cellar? But the Guest House didn't have a cellar. The Guest House, Barbara stopped suddenly as memory came flooding back. Hilda Hopkins had hit her. Her throat hurt, had the woman tried to strangle her as well. She squatted on her haunches and ran her fingers round her throat. It felt swollen, and was sore to the touch. Further memories hit her, the smell of decaying flesh, that was what she could smell in here. She recoiled in horror, this was a charnel house. Barbara dropped back onto all fours and scurried towards the light ignoring the rough feel of the floor beneath her knees. Her breath was coming in short sharp gasps, she was hyperventilating. She mustn't panic. She stopped and crouched by the entrance, fighting to make her breathing even. She wanted to scream but her throat was too sore.

Barbara realised she was at the entrance to a cave. Where was it? How high up the cliff was she, would it flood at high tide? No, the floor was bone dry, there was no sea weed, surely a tidal cave would be damp. Cautiously Barbara peered through the rough entrance. There was something in front of it. She put her hand forward then squealed and drew it back sharply, gasping as thorns ripped across the back of it. Brambles? Not here, she strove to keep her mind focused. Gorse, the headland had been dotted with gorse bushes. She tried moving forward again, easing herself through the hole, but keeping her back to the cliff, was this a ledge, how wide was it? How far up?

Barbara's nose wrinkled. She had expected the air to be fresh once she had left the cave, but there was a strong smell of smoke. It was heavy, not a barbecue, something much bigger. Barbara looked up the cliff face, wincing as pain shot through her head. There was a glow. Something was on fire, something large and she could hear the crackling of the flames now above the sound of the surf.

Something was tickling her chest. She lifted her tee shirt, forgetting that she had been about to get in the bath and was wearing no underwear. There was something on her skin. Lots of somethings in fact, off white, fat and round, like caterpillars…. Maggots… she had maggots crawling all over her. They must have come off the body in the cave. Thankfully for her peace of mind, Barbara did not know at that time how many bodies were piled up in the cavern. None the less she squealed and swept them off with her hands. She pulled the tee shirt over her head and used it to scrub her back. She crouched against the ground, shaking and shaking the top until she was sure there were no more maggots left, before pulling it back over her head. In her agitation she pulled it on back to front, the back neckline caught her across her sore throat. She leant back against the cliff face. "Get a grip Barbara, take it off, and dress properly." She found she was speaking out loud, berating herself, she breathed deeply and steadied herself.

Barbara's eyes were becoming used to the gloom. She realised she was on a pathway which went up and down the cliff from this point. Should she go down to the beach, would Hopkins be waiting at the top for her, or was the woman convinced she had killed her? She strained her ears, she could hear surf pounding below her. The tide must be in, she would have to go up.

Barbara clung to the side of the cliff. She had a good head for heights, but between her injured head and the darkness, shot now and then by flickering orange lights, she felt distinctly dizzy. She realised this must be the cliff path opposite to the Travellers' Rest. The one with the warning sign advising folk not to venture down it. If she was right about what was squirreled away in the cave, the woman wouldn't have wanted anyone coming across it accidentally. How the devil had she found it in the first place?

Barbara dropped to all fours again and crept up the final few feet of the path, peering along the headland to see if anyone was around. She stopped dead as she caught sight of the Guest House. She had known subconsciously that it must be this that was alight, but it was still a shock to see the place being consumed by flames.

She staggered across the headland towards the building. The flames had reached the roof now and were licking around the chimneys. Barbara stood, appalled and fascinated. She looked up at the top floor. There was a figure behind the window, banging on it. Barbara made out the shape of a woman, mouth agape in a silent scream, silent here; she was probably making more than enough noise up there, white hair plastered across her face. Barbara had barely registered the figure when the window blew out, the roof caved in and the figure fell backwards into the maul of the house in a welter of sparks.

Barbara sank to her knees, tears streaming down her face. Relief, fear, revulsion, she didn't know what emotions were surging through her. She had to do something. She was still a police officer, she had to take charge. Of what, she thought, a body in a cave and a funeral pyre? The tears changed to laughter which rapidly became hysterical. She fell forward, beating the earth with her hands.

Twin headlights pierced the darkness as a car accelerated up to the house. A door slammed and Graham Perkins raced towards the conflagration screaming Barbara's name.

"I'm here. I'm here," it came out as a croak, but Graham spun round on his heel and scanned the headland behind him. She had started laughing again, like a maniac, she knew it was ridiculous but she couldn't stop.

Graham scooted across to her. He took in the situation in a moment, grasped her by the shoulder and used his other hand to strike her sharply across the cheek.

The laughter ceased abruptly, and Barbara lay weakly in his grip.

"I couldn't stop. I'm sorry. Oh Graham, I saw her at the window. The Hopkins woman. She's still in there."

"Hilda Hopkins?"

"Yes, she was in the kitchen. She must have been holed up here Graham. It was definitely her, I'll never forget that face. She attacked me and dumped me in a cave down there." She pointed towards the cliff path, "There's another body in there, the smell is sickening, and there were maggots. She must be in league with the Moffat woman, it must have taken both of them to move me down there."

Graham looked across at the building.

"Well she's burning in hell now Barbara, it's over."

He fished out his mobile. There was no signal.

"Come on, we'll have to go down the coast road to get a signal. I need to get the Fire Brigade out here."

He paused, and used his hand to flick something out of Barbara's hair. Barbara shuddered and ran her hands across her head.

"What is it? There were maggots Graham, they're not still on me?" her voice rose in panic.

"No, they're all gone. You're fine."

Barbara leant against his chest.

"I want to get under a shower, for a long, long time."

Graham gave her a reassuring hug and looked back towards the house.

"Did you see the other one in the fire? The landlady, Moffat?"

Barbara glanced towards the lean to.

"No, I reckon she panicked after she realised what Hopkins had done, made a run for it. Her car's gone. I didn't see her earlier, only Hopkins, and I don't think she can drive. And it was Hopkins who attacked me. The other one must have come in later and helped her to move me." She shuddered again, "I think Hopkins guessed I'd recognised her."

Chapter 22

Graham Perkins and Barbara Grey revisited the site in the morning. Barbara had a large dressing on her forehead, and her right hand was wrapped in bandages. She was wearing one of Graham's shirts and a pair of leggings given to her by one of the nurses who worked in Casualty. Her throat was dreadfully stiff and sore, and she held herself carefully as she looked at the burnt ruins of the Guest House. By the time they had managed to contact the Fire Brigade there hadn't been much left for them to do other than to damp down the smouldering remains and remove a blackened object, curled up into a foetal position, from the ashes.

That had been taken off to the mortuary in Danemouth where in due course comparison with dental records would identify it as Hilda Beatrice Hopkins. There was no sign of Abigail Moffat, only her car, crumpled into a tangled mess of metal at the foot of the cliffs. It looked as if she had become disorientated and driven over the cliff edge. There was no trace of a body, but as the Coastguard had said, with the currents and races along this part of the coast it could wash up anywhere. The car was closely inspected, there was no evidence of the money which had been drawn out of the bank either, just a suitcase stuffed with Barbara Grey's belongings, now soiled and damp with sea water. The secret of the money had apparently died with the two old women.

Epilogue

Hilda Hopkins perused the headlines outlining the tragedy in the newspaper. She smiled quietly to herself as she read the reports of her own demise. The bodies had all been recovered from the cave, and subsequently identified. However there had been no trace of Abigail Moffat. Of course not, she thought scornfully, she was buried in the local churchyard in a pauper's grave under Hilda's name. Hilda checked the rolls of banknotes in her handbag. What she needed now was a new identity, and a passport. She rather fancied a trip on the Orient Express to Venice. She hadn't been abroad before, but the Orient Express had always fascinated her, and it would be good to get away from England for a few months.

Hilda Hopkins, Domi-Knit-Rix

Vivienne Fagan

Dedicated to my Bingo partner, Karen, in the hope that we win the big one!

Chapter 1

The Orient Express was champing at its bit, straining to depart from London Victoria Station in all its olde world glory. Recently engaged Police officers, Barbara Grey and Graham Perkins, gazed at it in awe. Barbara was bubbling over with excitement, hopping from foot to foot like an excited child. Graham Perkins watched her affectionately. They were going to have a lovely break, one that they would normally never have been able to afford on police pay. Barbara, being at a loose end one evening, had accompanied her friend Karen to a bingo hall, and they had won the jackpot. Even allowing for their pact to share any winnings fifty-fifty, it had amounted to a considerable sum. Most of Barbara's win was destined to go into savings towards the deposit for a house, but she had decided to give herself and Graham the trip of a lifetime as a special treat.

Barbara, smiling at the steward who was to look after them on the journey, climbed up the steps into their designated carriage. Graham scrambled up after her. The pair eagerly inspected their compartment. Barbara returned to the corridor very impressed, leaving Graham to test the softness of the seats. The train was now minutes away from departure, and even though no-one was seeing them off, Barbara just wanted to watch as they left the station.

'It's wonderful,' she thought to herself.

Barbara moved to one side as a tardy passenger clambered up the steps, followed by a harassed looking porter. The porter almost threw a set of luggage through into the neighbouring compartment.

"Just in time, madam," he said, dropping the suitcases higgledy-piggledy onto the floor and hurrying to step back down onto the platform "there you go, I don't want to be trapped on here when the doors are closed."

"The taxi got stuck in traffic. I thought I was going to miss the train," replied the woman grimly, "there would have been trouble if he hadn't got here when he did."

Barbara glanced across to the doorway. Don't say they were going to have an old misery guts as a neighbour. This was a four day trip and she didn't want anything to spoil it.

The two women's gaze met, and recognition flared in Hilda Hopkins' eyes. Barbara was a little slower on the uptake, after all, she genuinely believed that Hilda Hopkins was dead and buried.

"Graham," Barbara called sharply, "Graham, come here. Now!"

Hilda Hopkins turned, barging past Barbara, knocking her off balance as she scrambled down the steps of the carriage in the wake of the porter. The door slid across and locked as the train began its journey. Hilda stood on the platform, catching her breath and staring up at the window as the train moved off, before turning sharply on her heel and heading for the station entrance.

Graham rushed into the corridor just as Barbara staggered to her feet and put her hand out towards the emergency cord. He took hold of her, staying her hand, and asked,

"What is it?"

"The Hopkins woman," shrilled Barbara, "I've just seen her. She was next door. She isn't dead, Graham."

Graham pulled her back into their compartment and forcibly sat her down on the seat.

"What are you on about? You know she's dead, you saw her die in the fire."

Graham was concerned. Barbara had nearly been killed by Hilda Hopkins. She had been left for dead in a cave which already contained six bodies, and had arrived back at the guesthouse in time to see an elderly woman being consumed by the flames which were destroying the building. At the time the woman was believed to be the serial killer, Hilda Hopkins, while her erstwhile partner, Abigail Moffat, was thought to have drowned after her car went over the cliff. Her body had never been found.

Graham looked worriedly at Barbara. She had been through a lot, and had spent several weeks receiving counselling. She appeared to have come through the whole terrible experience relatively unscathed; what was this, some sort of delayed shock or breakdown?

"She recognised me, Graham. She just jumped off the train. Why would she do that if it wasn't her?"

Graham was in a quandary. What to do? The train had picked up speed and if it was Hilda Hopkins back at Victoria, he doubted that she would have hung around waiting to see what happened. He stood up and left the compartment. He inspected the neighbouring suite, it was empty except for two suitcases in a bright red tartan. Red tartan, hadn't the Hopkins woman chosen that pattern before? When she went on some coach trip or other?

Graham pressed the bell on the wall and moments later the steward appeared.

"Do you know who these belong to?" asked Graham, flashing his warrant card and pointing at the set of tartan suitcases.

"It's a bit odd, Sir," replied the steward, looking worried, "it's not something I've had happen to me before. I just saw the passenger leap off the train while the doors were closing. I've been trying to contact the guard but I reckon he must be busy. She left all this behind. Do you think we need to stop the train and get the bomb squad on board?"

"Not the bomb squad," said Graham, "but this luggage needs to be taken off and delivered to the police at the earliest opportunity."

"That'll be Dover, Sir."

"Fair enough. Can you lock this door please?" he pulled out his mobile phone, "I need to get in touch with my senior officer."

Hilda Hopkins paused in her headlong flight towards the station entrance. She had to get away from the area, not go wandering round the streets out there. She was less than a mile from New Scotland Yard, time to change direction. She fed coins into a ticket machine, and bought herself a one day travel card before heading towards the nearest underground entrance and jumping on the first train which appeared.

Chapter 2

Claire Naylor put down her phone and went to tap on Detective Inspector John Brent's door.

"It's about the cases from Merrydown Crescent and Grimes Cove, Guv," she explained. "You know the one, Hilda Hopkins, the machine knitting killer."

Brent sat back in his chair and regarded Naylor curiously.

"The woman's dead and buried, Claire, months ago."

"They are exhuming the body from Grimes Cove churchyard. It appears that it might not be her interred there, they want to do DNA tests. It was only id'd on dental records apparently," she paused before dropping her bombshell, "Hilda Hopkins has been spotted in London, trying to get on the Orient Express."

"The Orient Express? Isn't that the train young Perkins and his girlfriend have gone off on?"

"Yes, Guv. It was PC Grey who spotted her. She was getting onto the train, Hopkins I mean, and Grey met her face to face. Well, as you can imagine, Hopkins' face is not one that Grey is likely to forget in a hurry."

Brent grimaced. Hilda Hopkins had come within an inch of murdering Barbara Grey when she had inadvertently stumbled across Hopkins' hideaway while on holiday. And now she had met up with her again, the young woman seemed to be jinxed, Brent thought ruefully.

"So where are they now?"

"Continuing their four days away, Guv. Perkins arranged to have Hopkins' luggage collected at Dover, but there wasn't much point in spoiling their break."

"Fair enough. I'd sooner have them back bright eyed and bushy tailed in a few days time than see them moping around here like kids denied a treat. Keep me abreast of what happens, Claire. There's going to be some questions asked if it does turn out she's alive and kicking. What's with this woman, she has the very luck of the devil."

"Tell me about it, Guv."

"I'll leave it in your capable hands, Claire, I promised Shirley I'd be home early today."

Claire left the office and headed back to her desk, what next she wondered, would the London police track Hopkins down quickly?

Chapter 3

"I'm home, Shirley". John Brent hung his coat on its peg in the hallway and went into the living room. A small boy sat on the hearth rug, lining up a group of toy cars, each one the same distance behind the other.

Brent ruffled the boy's head.

"Hello Duncan. Look at Dad, say hello."

The nine year old looked up, and fixed his eyes on the blank television screen.

"Say hello", he echoed.

Brent squatted down in front of the child and looked straight into his eyes,

"I'm over here Duncan" he said encouragingly.

Shirley Brent came in, drying her hands on a tea towel.

"That's good timing, dinner's about ready. Duncan,"

She paused as the boy glanced in her direction, then made a pantomime of washing her hands, "wash hands Duncan. Dinner time."

She sighed, and looked at her husband, "he's been good today, no autistic strops. Let's hope it continues."

Brent rose to his feet and gave her a hug.

"You remember that case we had, in Merrydown Crescent, the Hopkins woman?"

"The one who attacked Babs Grey? The machine knitting serial killer?"

"Yes indeed. Well, she's been resurrected. Or rather, she's never been dead. Forensics are doing DNA tests on the body in her grave, but chances are it will turn out to be the Moffat woman. They never did find her body despite having a good search for it. Hopkins is on the loose again."

"Oh no, around Midchester?"

"Hopefully she's not headed our way. She disappeared in London. Oddly enough it was young Grey who spotted her. Must have given her one hell of a shock. She's a damn good officer too; I don't want her being ruined by the likes of Hopkins."

"She meets criminals every day," pointed out Shirley.

"True, but she probably doesn't expect all of them to hit her over the head, strangle her then dump her in a hole full of dead bodies. Where's Duncan, he's very quiet?"

"Oh no," Shirley hurried out of the room. Water was cascading down the stairs from the bathroom.

Duncan was sitting on the top step, splashing his hands in the flow, a happy smile on his face.

"Wash hands, Duncan," he lisped.

Brent forgot about Hilda Hopkins and work as he rushed around with towels and mops helping his wife to clear up.

Chapter 4

Hilda Hopkins was also thinking about the Midchester Police. She had soon settled into her new bed sitting room. Now she was starting to relax and to ruminate. She didn't believe it. After all this time! It must be a good four months since she had left Barbara Grey for dead in a cave while she burnt down the Travellers' Rest Guest House to cover her tracks. It had worked too. Abigail Moffat had been buried under Hilda's name, and Hilda had been living very quietly, completely incognito.

Hilda's ambition had been to have a trip on the Orient Express. She had earmarked some of her ill gotten gains to this end. Hilda needed a new identity for a passport, she could hardly apply for one with her own details. She'd given it some thought. It was possible to get a new identity she knew, she had seen done in a film, what was it, oh yes, "The Day of the Jackal". The chappie in that story had searched churchyards looking for the graves of dead children who would now be around his own age. Hilda found this distinctly distasteful. However, she vaguely recollected her Aunt Joan and Uncle Bill Baxter, now long dead. Their only child, a girl who was two years younger than Hilda, had died of meningitis while still a toddler.

Hilda had tracked down her cousin's birth certificate and now had a passport in the name of Beryl Baxter. What a good job, she had reflected, that her father's sister had married a Mr Baxter. Hilda's maiden name was Sheepshanks, and she didn't want to be saddled with that name again. Anyway, she had thought, it was good to keep the name in the family; she wouldn't have felt comfortable using any dead person's identity. Hilda had no living family remaining, except possibly the husband who had deserted her decades ago, so, she reckoned in her own twisted way, there was no harm done.

But of course the train tickets had been in Beryl's name. The Police would check that first, the name of the fleeing passenger, should she hang onto the passport or not? Hilda sighed, she was getting too old for this sort of excitement. And what were the odds that she should meet Barbara Grey of all people? She couldn't believe it, talk about "Play it again Sam", and it wasn't even Casablanca, she hadn't even made it out of Victoria Station! All her lovely clothes and the smart set of luggage were on the train too. She wouldn't see them again.

'Don't cry over spilt milk, Hilda' she had told herself sharply, 'what's done is done. Time for plan B.'

Except she didn't have a plan B, not until she had quite unexpectedly spotted an ad for a maid.

The last thing Hilda had expected to happen was to nearly get caught just getting onto the train. She slipped off her shoes. Of course her presence of mind had allowed her to escape. She was still the best, the powers that shaped her mind were as sharp as ever. She just had to make sure she kept on top of things, and she had to continue to outmanoeuvre the police force. She swung her legs onto the bed and lay back.

What now? She had lost all her clothes, again. She had never managed to keep any decent clothes for long over the past few years, she reflected bitterly. She would have to see what she could find tomorrow at this dress agency that her new employer, Doreen Morgan, known professionally as Madame Tempest, had recommended.

'Moira's Modes', it sounded a bit old-fashioned, still she wasn't looking for trendy mini skirts and the likes at her age. She had been worried that she would be required to wear something like a French Maid's costume. That had actually been in Madame's mind, until, that is, she had met Hilda in the flesh. Hilda had put the weight back on which she had lost, plus an extra few pounds, and her silhouette was distinctly toad like. Madame had decided that something a little more conservative would look a lot less ridiculous.

Hilda brooded about her lost holiday. It was that Barbara Grey's fault. She had had the chance to do away with her, and she had messed it up, Barbara Grey had survived. She should have strangled Barbara and hidden her in her compartment, then dumped her from the moving train. But that wasn't viable, the sensible part of Hilda's brain told her. The compartments on the Orient Express weren't designed to have space for hidden bodies, and safety measures would prevent any doors being opened while the train was moving. Still, it was a nice thought, revenge and safety, a good combination. Despite her belief that she was too clever to get caught, Hilda still had a nagging respect for the Police. They were tenacious; they wouldn't give up until she was back in custody. It was time to disappear again, and hopefully this house would do very nicely just for now.

Chapter 5

The fog hung in wispy tendrils along the drab dead end road. It covered the roofs of the tall terraced houses, and slid over the edge of the railway bridge which fringed this street, aptly named, Railway Cuttings. The sounds of the trains passing by were muffled, lost in the murk and gloom as they chugged towards Marshchapel Street, the local railway station.

Number six was a rambling Victorian terraced house in this, one of the more salubrious streets which bordered the railway line. The buildings were clad in Virginia creeper whose leaves covered the front walls and snaked along the pipes and gutters. The paint on many of the window frames and front doors was flaking off, showing the bare untreated wood underneath. The street had an overall air of neglect, while at the same time hinting at a faded grandeur which sadly, it had never actually possessed.

Inside number six, the end of terrace house, which nestled adjacent to the railway bridge, Hilda Hopkins was working away diligently at her knitting machine. She had established it in the corner of the small bed sitting room she inhabited on the ground floor. Through the half open door she could occasionally hear a swish and a thwack, punctuated by cries of woe, as her employer, Madame Tempest gave her current client a good seeing to.

Hilda, with her customary devilish luck, had fallen into this job as live in Maid to a Mistress purely by accident. She had fled from Victoria Station after Barbara Grey had recognised her, taking the first underground train out of there that she could find. Emerging into the High Street several Boroughs away, Hilda had been alarmed to see two Police Community Support Officers heading her way. She had ducked into a telephone box on the pretence of making a call. On the wall were several sleazy advertisements, one of which had "Maid wanted" scrawled along the bottom, together with a phone number. Hilda pushed coins into the pay box, angling her body so that she could watch the progress of the PCSO's. They had strolled past the kiosk, completely ignoring her.

Hilda's telephone call had paid dividends. She had renamed herself Hildegarde Lamb, the Lamb being a play on her maiden name, and enquired if the Maid's job was still available? The voice at the other end of the phone had regretted that that particular job was now filled, but if Hilda really needed a place, well, there was always Madame Tempest if Hilda wasn't too fussy about the in-house activities? Hilda couldn't afford to be fussy, and in her innocence she didn't really know what the woman was driving at anyway. Hilda had taken down the number, called on the off chance and had found herself with a position and live in accommodation at the house of Madame Tempest, a dominatrix for special gentlemen. There was the added bonus that Madame hadn't seen it necessary to inform the tax or DWP people that she had an employee. Hilda had obtained a room, the run of the ground floor and cash in hand. It was ideal.

So now she was Maid to Madame Tempest, no questions asked. It was perfect. Madame Tempest had run through Hilda's duties. She was to meet and greet the clients, and accept Madame's tributes. Hilda had looked puzzled.

"The clients will give you a plain envelope, Hildegarde, which contains the payment for my services. It is called my tribute. Just keep it safe until I have finished, then you can give it to me. It just ensures that I don't have any money lying around where I am working."

Hilda was also to deliver the clients, once they had changed into their role play costumes, to the relevant room. Madame Tempest had two playrooms, a Headmistress' Study and a Dungeon. The Dungeon, like the Study, was on the first floor, which Hilda found a little odd, she had always associated dungeons with basements in castles. It was all proving to be something of a learning curve for Hilda including finding out that BDSM stood for Bondage, Discipline, Sadism and Masochism.

Hilda's experiences over the past few years had left her broad minded to a good extent, and she didn't much care what happened in this house so long as she was simply an onlooker. She had no strong wishes to take part in the proceedings whatsoever. Hilda understood that she was also there as a safety measure. There was less chance of Madame being attacked by a disgruntled punter if there was a witness on the premises.

Not that she would be that much good as a witness, Hilda thought to herself. Anything untoward that might cause the police to come calling would have her disappearing over the horizon in seconds flat. However she had no intention of letting Madame know this, she simply agreed to the stated duties. Madame didn't seem to be surprised that Hilda had no belongings with her and Hilda had not offered any explanation, better not to get entangled in a web of lies she had thought.

Madame Tempest's speciality, it transpired, was to cater for grown men who liked to revert to the happiest days of their life and have their bottoms smacked. Hilda had thought this an odd concept, but all Madame Tempest's clients were well over twenty one years of age, none of them was dragged in screaming off the street, and everything was consensual. Hilda was quite content to turn a blind eye, different stokes for different folks she had thought with a giggle when she first found out what the business was here.

Madame had suggested that Hildegarde should put a very light beige colour onto her hair. Hilda had done so. It took years off her appearance. She had bought a pair of tortoiseshell rimmed glasses with plain lenses, although Hilda actually had excellent eyesight for her age. The change in her appearance from these simple measures had been striking. For work, Madame Tempest had decided that Hilda should wear a crisp white blouse, teamed with a black skirt, and she looked the very epitome of a personal assistant.

There had been a heart stopping test for her new appearance too. Amongst Madame's clientele there were several faces which Hilda found vaguely familiar. Madame insisted on absolute discretion, and Hilda had been trained not to betray recognition of any celebrity by as much as a blink. This training had held her in good stead when she opened the door one day and found a man on the doorstep who she instantly recognised. The last time she had seen him, he had been dressed in red robes and was remanding her into custody at the Crown Court. He scarcely glanced at Hilda, he was eager to get into the premises and away from the road. Hilda showed him into the small dressing room before taking him upstairs to Madame's study, neatly dressed in schoolboy uniform, complete with short grey trousers and a school cap.

"Matthews, you revolting little boy, remove your cap when you enter into my presence."

Hilda didn't wait to hear the response. She closed the door and retired downstairs, heart still palpitating. She didn't understand the psychology behind the man's need to be disciplined, but if it kept her in bread and butter, and out of the public eye, it was all to the good.

She went back to her room. It was a small bed sitting room at the front of the house. Hilda had bought a knitting machine through an advertisement in a machine knitting magazine and she was well content. Out of caution, she rarely left the house other than to do messages and the odd bit of shopping at Madame's behest. Madame mainly kept to her own quarters upstairs, although the two women shared meals which Hilda cooked in the small kitchen diner to the rear of the house. Their relationship was purely employer/employee, and no hint of friendship hung between them.

This suited Hilda very well. She had been forced to do away with Abigail Moffat, her partner and companion at the Travellers' Rest Guest House when she felt that Abigail was becoming unglued. Hilda still had the odd pang of remorse about this act, Abigail was the closest to a friend that she had ever had, and she didn't want to get so close to another human being ever again. If it came to them or her, Hilda knew exactly who would come out of the conflict alive.

She heard the door open upstairs, and a pattering on the steps as "Master" Matthews came back downstairs to change into his normal clothes. Hilda hovered by her door. She had to let him out through the front door, before closing up for the night.

Madame Tempest strolled downstairs just as Hilda was shooting the bolts home. She glanced into Hilda's room as she went along to the kitchen. A half finished piece of knitting hung from the knitting machine. Madame paused, and looked more closely at the machine.

"I've an idea Hildegarde, it could mean a few extra bob for you too. Come and have a coffee."

"I don't drink coffee, I'll be along in a moment, Madame, and make myself a cup of tea."

Hilda went across to the machine and removed the weights which were hanging from the knitted fabric. She didn't want the stitches being distorted. She touched the machine gently before making her way to the kitchen.

Madame had made her coffee, and the water was back on the boil for Hilda's tea. She took her cup to the table and sat down, eager to hear about this new money making idea.

"I have some clients who are interested in infantilism," said Madame Tempest.

Hilda looked puzzled. It was a term which was new to her.

"A lot of my clients like to role play as schoolboys, usually wearing a near replica of the uniform they wore at their prep schools."

Hilda nodded, she didn't see the point of this herself, but it behooved her to keep her opinions to herself if she wanted to stay here.

"Some like to regress further, to a younger age. Either young toddlers or babies."

"Oh, right", replied Hilda, thinking that she had heard everything now. She hadn't of course, but Madame Tempest didn't usually dip her toe into the very extremes of BDSM.

"That machine of yours, have you ever done baby clothes on it?"

"Not this one, but I've made baby things in the past," replied Hilda.

"Could you make baby bonnets to fit grown up heads? And baby or toddler clothes in large sizes?"

Hilda pondered the problem for a few minutes.

"Yes, I should think so," she said at last, "it's just a matter of adjusting the size. I can easily do jumpers with cute bunnies or kittens or whatever on them."

"What about dresses, or buster suits?"

"Buster suits, do you mean jumpers with knitted shorts?"

Madame Tempest nodded.

"I should think so, I could draw some diagrams for the knitradar on the machine and work from them."

"Think about it, Hildegarde. Maybe try out a couple of garments, let's see how you do."

"What sort of sizes are we looking at?" asked Hilda, "Your clientele come in a wide range, the ones I've seen anyway."

"Well, you know Matthews? He was here this afternoon, he wears a burgundy and gold uniform?"

Hilda nodded, keeping her face completely expressionless. She had met Master Matthews in his adult persona; the man was a Crown Court Judge, the Right Honourable Tarquin Cressingham-Gore.

"I know he would just love a jumper with a train chugging along the front. A steam train, not a modern day one of course."

"I could make one with a train and carriages on the front, and continue the carriages partway round the back too, and put some clouds in the sky, make it into a proper picture jumper?"

"And a smiley sun?"

"Yes and a smiley sun."

"Go for it Hildegarde, how long will that take you?"

"A couple of days to knit it, another day to sew it up," replied Hilda.

"A day to sew it up?"

"Making up is the most important, you can ruin a good piece of knitting with careless stitching," Hilda was ever the perfectionist when it came to her knitting.

"Whatever," Madame was getting bored, "just have a go at it Hildegarde and let me see the finished article."

It had worked out very nicely. Hilda had a good eye for colour, and she turned out some stunning juvenile knitwear in adult sizes. The very novelty guaranteed that she was able to secure a good price for her garments. Matthews had been almost incandescent with delight when he had seen his train jumper.

Hilda guessed that Madame added her own cut to the finished price; the garments were always sold through her and not Hilda. An extra envelope was added to the tribute stack for each purchased garment and Madame handed out Hilda's share of the money without telling her the original selling price. Hilda however was quite content to simply add banknotes to her growing account, the money was secondary to the pleasure she got from designing and knitting the clothes in the first place.

She had watched Malcolm, one of the clients who liked to regress to his toddler days, going into Madame's dungeon. Malcolm was neatly dressed in navy blue knitted shorts with a matching navy blue sailor top, complete with a square white nautical collar and cheeky red bow. She smiled to herself, Hilda Hopkins Domi-Knit-Rix, that was an apt description for her!

Chapter 6

Clive Barcroft stopped at the second window in the drive thru and accepted two bags of hamburgers and chips and two milkshakes. He passed them to his team partner, Barbara Grey, and they drove about a mile down the road before parking in a layby. Barbara was thirsty and poked the straw impatiently into the paper cup before taking a long gulp.

"Scrummy, Clive," she murmured. She took a bite out of the hamburger, wiping onion and lettuce off the side of her mouth.

"We had some fantastic meals while we were away, but give me good old hamburger and chips on a late shift", she grinned.

"You haven't brought your photos in yet, Barb, Lillian keeps asking me if you have any. She reckons we need to start saving now and go off on a luxury trip when the kids are old enough to look after themselves."

"She's not got her sights set on next year then?"

Clive's son Angus was six, and his daughter Morag was four. Barcroft laughed,

"If ever, it might be a nice pipe dream. Did you have a good time though, once you'd crossed the Channel?"

"You mean once I knew that we didn't have a serial killer in the next compartment?" asked Barbara ruefully, "I'll tell you what Clive, I'm getting distinctly paranoid about arranging any more holidays. I might try and make the next one an 18-35, just so that there's no chance of me coming nose to nose with the Hopkins woman again!"

"And they've no idea where she disappeared to?"

"Nope, not a trace. Probably turned herself into a bat and flew off into the sunset."

Barbara swallowed the last of the hamburger, and looked impishly at Barcroft.

"Of course the ideal solution would have been to have had the Hopkins woman found in her compartment, stabbed lots of times by all the relatives of her victims who just happened to be travelling on the train as well."

"And Monsieur Poirot of course," chuckled Barcroft, following her thinking.

"It would make an excellent story," added Barbara wistfully, "if Agatha Christie hadn't already written it!"

Barcroft stuffed the empty containers back into a carrier bag. Graham Perkins had asked him how he felt Barbara was coping, and from this little episode Barcroft reckoned that she was well and truly back on track again. She was a good professional officer, and Barcroft felt that Barbara's horrific experiences had only added to her strength and determination.

They sat in a companionable silence for several minutes, each engrossed in their own thoughts.

"Oh well, this won't keep the burglars at bay," murmured Barcroft. He slipped the car into gear and drove off, back on patrol.

Chapter 7

Hilda was out shopping for food when the house was raided. She strolled along the road, pulling her shopping trolley behind her and turned into the street approaching Railway Cuttings. The road was cordoned off with blue tape. Hilda faltered for a minute before continuing on her way. It would look odd if she did a sudden about turn. As she approached the junction a young policeman glanced at her, but she made no attempt to go into Railway Cuttings, merely slowing down just before she crossed the road.

"What's happening down there?" she asked, as the policeman looked down at her, "has there been an accident?"

"Nothing for you to worry about, ma'am", replied the policeman, "just a raid on a er," he looked at the dowdy elderly woman, "er, a house down there. Nothing to worry yourself about," he repeated, turning away from her without a second glance.

Hilda continued down the road towards a small Journey Lodge hotel which was situated not far from the railway station. She booked herself in, and wondered what was going to happen next. She had sufficient money with her to keep her for a few days, and quite a considerable amount more squirreled away. All her machine knitting paraphernalia was still in her bed sitting room at 6 Railway Cuttings. Would that raise alarm bells with any of those police officers? She hoped not, after all she couldn't be the only woman in London whose hobby was machine knitting.

Hilda dug her diary out of her bag. It had a phone number which Madame had given her in case of emergencies. The number belonged to June, the woman who had first steered Hilda in Madame Tempest's direction. Hilda picked up the receiver and dialled. June answered.

"The house has been raided. The police are still there and I don't know what's happened to Madame Tempest."

"Don't worry Hildegarde, that is Hildegarde?"

Hilda confirmed her identity.

"It happens once or twice a year, when the Vice Squad are at a loose end. Doreen will ring her solicitor and he will arrange bail. She'll probably just get a fine at the Magistrates' Court for running a disorderly house or some such charge, then she'll be home again."

"I wish she had explained this to me," complained Hilda, "I had a hell of a shock when I saw the Police all round there."

"Don't worry about it," replied the other woman, "have you got somewhere to stay?"

"I'm in……." Hilda's natural caution kicked in, "I've got a room away from there."

"Give it twenty four hours then you can go back."

"Won't they realise there is someone else staying there? In my room I mean?"

"With all due respect, it's Doreen they are interested in, the Madame, they don't usually bother with the hired help unless they think you are involved with the doings."

Hilda had scowled when being referred to as the hired help, but her resentment was overlaid with relief.

"No, apart from my knitting I don't have any contact with the clients, other than letting them in and letting them out again and collecting Madame's tributes of course."

"You just relax, enjoy an evening off. The place will be back to normal tomorrow you'll see, although the clients may take a couple of weeks to pop their heads over the parapet if they see Madame's name in the paper."

Chapter 8

"Claire, I've got a job for you." DI John Brent put his head round the door of his office and called out to DS Naylor, "Come in here a minute."

"What's up Guv?" she asked, taking the chair opposite his desk.

"I need you to do a liaison job for me. There's a woman panicking about Hilda Hopkins being on the loose. Seems to think that she will be murdered in her bed if she comes back here."

"But that's a job for Witness Protection", protested Claire.

"She's asked specifically for you. Seems she only trusts you." He grimaced.

Claire looked at him sharply.

"Oh no, it's not Lettice and her mother is it Guv?"

"Got it in one Claire. That's what makes you such a good detective, instinct." He grinned.

"Yeah, right Guv. The woman's a pain in the neck. Mrs Leverson I mean, not Lettice. I bet Lettice hasn't made any complaints at all, not on her own behalf, it'll be Mother who doesn't like it."

"Nip along and see them. Give then some reassurance. I can't see that they are in any danger from Hopkins. If she had anything against Lettice she would have done away with her years ago, when they were on that coach excursion. You can take young Perkins along with you if it makes you feel any better," he added with a wicked grin.

"I'll take you up on that, Guv," she replied, "I'm sure he will be thrilled to meet Mother again."

In the event the visit wasn't as traumatic as Claire had feared. She rang the bell of the neat townhouse and looked along the quiet avenue. Lettice opened the door, with Mother behind her sitting in her wheelchair. Claire had a distinct sense of déjà vu. Mrs Leverson glided forward and peered past Claire into the street.

"It's a plain car, Mrs Leverson," murmured Claire, "we are being discreet." She smiled at Miss Leverson, "good to see you again, Lettice."

"Come into the sitting room," said Mrs Leverson, it was a command more than an invitation, "just follow me. Lettice, tea, and don't forget my biscuits."

"That's all right….." began Graham.

"It's for me, not you. You are on duty aren't you young man?" interrupted Mrs Leverson. She steered herself into a large sitting room and did a U-turn until she was facing them again.

"Do sit down. We've been watching the television and we saw that Hilda Hopkins has been allowed to escape. I worry that she might come looking for Lettice. I don't want Lettice harmed, goodness knows what I'd do without her. She knows all my little ways, it would take weeks to train someone else."

She pushed her glasses back up her beaky nose and pursed her lips.

Claire fought to keep her face impassive. Her eyes fell on the lap rug tucked over Mrs Leverson's knees. She hadn't noticed it the last time she had been there. The centre was machine knitted in shades of blue and cream, and it had a pretty pink and cream floral pattern as a border.

"What a charming rug," Claire commented.

"Lettice made if for me. I find it very useful, it keeps my knees warm, I'm arthritic you know, but it's not so bulky as a normal blanket," explained Mrs Leverson, "there's one of those knitting machine clubs in the Community Centre where I go for my over 70's Coffee afternoon. Lettice takes me. When she saw that there was a knitting club there she decided she would like to join. She has some very independent ideas sometimes, gets it from her father, my late husband I suppose. My side of the family are much more accommodating. It's only once a month thankfully so she's able to accompany me for the rest of the time so I said she might as well go. It's worked out quite nicely actually, she's made me some very useful garments."

"Does she have a machine of her own then?"

"Oh yes, one of the women was selling her old machine and Lettice bought it. She even had the woman round here several times to get some tuition on it." Mrs Leverson sniffed.

Lettice pushed a hostess trolley into the room. It held a teapot, and a cup and saucer, a plate of biscuits and three glasses of lemonade.

Lettice shyly offered a tumbler of the cold drink to Claire,

"I make it myself," she twittered.

Claire smiled and took a sip of the lemonade. It really was delicious, she was surprised.

"That's very nice," she said sincerely. "Now, as to your concerns about Hilda Hopkins. We really don't expect her to return to this area. She was actually spotted in London, and we've no reason to think she wants to come back. Her house is boarded up and all her belongings are in storage, there's nothing here for her. Plus she's known down here, so chances are she will head further afield," she smiled reassuringly at the two women. Lettice was staring intently at her knees while Mrs Leverson appeared to be hanging on every word.

"I can leave you a card with my number in case you do have any worries. From what I understand she regarded Lettice as a friend, we don't think she would ever want to harm her. And she has no idea where Lettice lives does she?"

"I don't know what Lettice told her," snapped Mrs Leverson, "cavorting with a mass murderer indeed."

"We call them serial killers nowadays Mrs Leverson," interposed Graham.

Mrs Leverson regarded him through small, black piggy eyes.

"Quite."

Graham took a swig of his lemonade, and looked helplessly across at Claire. Lettice's head reared up,

"Mother! Of course I didn't tell her my address, we were only together for a couple of days."

"Anyway, I thought she was supposed to be dead," continued Mrs Leverson as if Lettice hadn't spoken, "didn't they bury her somewhere? How did she materialise again?"

"It wasn't her body in the grave, we believe it was her partner, Abigail Moffat, there'd been a mix up with some dental records."

"Incompetence," snapped Mrs Leverson, "surely they knew which one they had when they recovered the body?"

Claire sighed. Tactful words and euphemisms weren't going to work with this one. She glanced anxiously at Lettice sitting quietly to one side nibbling on a biscuit.

"The body had been burnt beyond visual recognition. The fire really was an inferno; it burnt down a whole building you know. They used dental records because there wasn't much else to go on. Plus someone had seen the woman at the window during the fire, only briefly, but she thought it was Hilda Hopkins so…."

"So they didn't look too closely. Just closed the case and were thankful to do so I suppose." Mrs Leverson replaced her cup on its saucer. "Very well, thank you for coming." It was clearly a dismissal.

"Lettice, see our visitors out. Put that card somewhere safe," she handed Claire's card to her daughter, "it would appear that we are not likely to be murdered in our beds after all. You do get some silly ideas Lettice."

"But Mother, it wasn't me, you said……" Lettice's voice faded away, and she turned to the two police officers.

"Thank you, I'll let you out."

They stood on the doorstep for a few minutes.

"I'm glad you got your knitting machine after all, Lettice," murmured Claire, "It looks as if you've got the hang of it very quickly."

"The ladies at the Club are very helpful, I come away from there brimming over with ideas," smiled Lettice, looking uncharacteristically animated. "I just love it. Did you ever get one, you said you might?"

"It's on the back burner at the minute," admitted Claire, "but I'm very tempted again. Anyway, keep that card safe. I doubt you will ever see Hilda Hopkins again, but of course if you did, we would appreciate a phone call."

"Lettice!"

Lettice Leverson closed her eyes momentarily, and stepped back inside, shutting the door firmly in Claire's face.

Chapter 9

Hilda had accompanied Madame to the Magistrates' Court at her behest. Hilda had been understandably reluctant to enter the portals of such a place but Madame had put her at her ease, and anyway, once they were nearly there, the two women had approached the Court independently.

"You sit in the Public Gallery, Hildegarde. It'll be useful for you to see what happens," Madame had grinned, "this is a sort of occupational hazard in this profession."

Hilda found herself a seat in the front row of the Gallery. She reckoned she may as well be bold. If she was in the lions' den, it was only right she should look the lions in the eye. No-one took the slightest notice of her. She stood with the rest of the spectators when the three Magistrates entered and took their places.

"Can you sit down missus," snapped a voice behind her.

"Sorry" mumbled Hilda, dropping back into her seat. She had been so transfixed she hadn't realised that everyone was sitting again. The Chairman of the Magistrates was someone who Hilda recognised. She had made a pale blue jumper for him, with a picture of a large pink rabbit eating a carrot on the front. She sat back in her seat, what would happen if he glanced up and spotted her?

Absolutely nothing as it turned out. Madame took her place in the dock looking suitably penitent. The Magistrate made several, in the event, hypocritical, comments about the running of a bawdy house. A fine was imposed and Madame left the courtroom.

Hilda met up with her in a café not far from the Court.

"But that was...." started Hilda....

"Discretion Hildegarde, what do I always say? Be a wise monkey, see nothing, hear nothing, say nothing."

Hilda swallowed a mouthful of tea.

"Did you know it was going to be....er ....him?" she asked.

"I had a fair idea. He'll get an extra drubbing for that fine, it was a bit hefty this time, but I dare say he'll enjoy that nonetheless."

Madame laughed. Hilda's mouth turned down at the corners, she still couldn't see the attraction of being whacked. Still, she brightened up, if Madame had a tame Magistrate on the go and a Crown Court Judge, it might make the place a bit more secure for herself in the long run.

"It's a pity you don't have the odd Chief Constable or two in your stable" grinned Hilda.

"And what makes you think I haven't? You've not met all the clients yet, Hildegarde."

Madame Tempest sipped her coffee and looked quizzically at Hilda.

"Why Hildegarde? Closest to Hilda I suppose." Madame answered her own question.

Hilda was knocked for six and looked it. She couldn't help it. The comment had come straight out of the blue.

"I saw your picture on the news the day you came to me. You had no luggage, were desperate for a job, and you called yourself Hildegarde.....obvious really."

Hilda bit her lip.

"What are you going to do?"

"Finish my coffee and get back home. You'll need to drink that up too. We've wasted enough time on this Court nonsense, and haven't you got a couple of jumpers to finish?"

"Do you mean...." Hilda couldn't finish the question.

"No skin off my nose, so long as you don't intend bumping off my clientele."

She raised an eyebrow.

"Of course not, most of the other ones were more or less accidental," Hilda responded faintly.

"Well then, that's sorted. I need a maid, Hilda, and you fill that post very nicely. I don't want you going looking for other employment."

"It never entered my head," Hilda replied truthfully enough, "I'm well suited where I am, Madame."

Chapter 10

"It's been confirmed, it's definitely Abigail Moffat in the Hopkins' grave."

Graham Perkins stood in the middle of the sitting room in Barbara's flat and took her into his arms.

"It seems fairly certain that it was Hilda Hopkins who you saw on the train."

Barbara pulled away impatiently.

"Of course it was her. Did you ever doubt it Graham? What is it, the little woman has flipped her bonnet, imagines any female over fifty-five must be Hilda Hopkins? Let's treat her with kid gloves in case she breaks in half? Men!"

Graham flinched. He had expected his news to upset Barbara but not in this way, where was this anger coming from?

"Well of course I believed you. I got them to take her luggage off the train remember. Come on Babs, don't shoot the messenger."

He turned away from her and collapsed onto the sofa.

"I surrender! Honest!"

Barbara sat down beside him.

"Sorry, I tend to get a bit paranoid about the blasted woman still, don't I?"

"John Brent suggested I come round and tell you. He wanted me to break it to you gently rather than you go into the nick and find out."

"I already knew in my own mind. Still, it's good to get confirmation, if only to let you lot in CID know that those of us in uniform have eyes too!"

"I never doubted it. Brent was thinking of you though, Barb, he's a good bloke you know."

"I suppose so," admitted Barbara cautiously. Detective Inspector Brent had given her a terrific reprimand on the day that Hilda Hopkins had first escaped. Barbara had been responsible for watching her but the wily woman had scrambled out of a cloakroom window and fled the scene.

"So what's happening now?"

"Well, her picture is going out all round the country. There's been no trace of her anywhere, goodness knows where she has gone to ground."

"Try matching any unsolved murders to her," suggested Barbara, "or do you think she has turned over a new leaf and is now knitting socks for the Women's Institute in some tiny village deep in the country?"

"It's an open case again. We'll just have to stay focused. Brent doesn't reckon she'll come back into our patch, and she was in London last time she was seen", he added unnecessarily. Barbara knew exactly where Hopkins had last been seen. "It's easy to disappear in a place like London. Nobody takes any notice of their neighbours there, or hardly ever."

He put his arm round Barbara's shoulder and gave her a hug.

"Am I forgiven?"

She laughed and hugged him back.

"I wonder why Brent wanted me to know before I went into the Station though," she said, "did he think I would burst into tears and run screaming into the Ladies?"

"Not at all," replied Graham firmly, "he's just being considerate Babs, he's that sort of chap. You got off on the wrong foot with him I know, but he's not one to bear grudges."

"So, it seems like I have two choices. I either emigrate to the Scottish Highlands, dig a hole and pull it in after me, or I dust off my truncheon and get out there to see if I can find the old witch."

"Don't go to Scotland Babs," laughed Graham, "you'll probably meet her taking Nessie for a walk."

Barbara chuckled, a mental picture of Hilda Hopkins walking along a path with the Loch Ness Monster on a collar and lead had formed in her mind.

"Perfect pet for her, I should think Graham, monsters squared!"

Chapter 11

The doorknocker hammered loudly on the front door. Hilda looked up from her knitting and checked the time. There was a client due in about half an hour, a chap called Edwin according to the appointment list, but no-one before that. She opened the door cautiously. Outside the rain was lashing out of the heavens, and a gust blew a wet spray into the hallway. Edwin stood there, looking damp and miserable.

"You're too early," hissed Hilda.

"What is it Hildegarde," called out Madame from upstairs.

"It's Master Edwin, Ma'am" replied Hilda, "he's early, it's pouring down with rain, can I let him in?"

"Oh yes, I suppose so, considering. Take him to the kitchen, I'm not ready for him yet. Give him a hot drink and a biscuit."

Hilda bustled about making tea, and tipped some biscuits onto a plate. Edwin eased his bulk onto a chair after shaking his upper torso like a terrier to dry himself. He gratefully accepted a cup of tea, shovelling three heaped teaspoons of sugar into it before he raised it to his lips. Hilda pushed the plate of biscuits across to him and settled down to drink her own tea.

The house vibrated slightly as a train passed close by. Edwin perked up.

"That'll be the 14:27 to Milton Magna," he announced.

"Pardon?"

Another train could be heard lumbering along the line.

"And that's a goods train going to the Power Station at North Bridgechester," he grinned at Hilda.

"I know all the timetables," he told her, "I used to work in a signalling box."

"Oh right," Hilda murmured faintly.

"They are all automatic now of course. But, you know, I've travelled all over the country. You could put me down blindfolded on any part of the train system and I could tell from the feel of the ballast between the rails where we were."

He looked at her as if he expected her to take him up on his boast but Hilda merely stretched out her hand and picked up a biscuit. Another train clattered past the house. This prompted Edwin to start reciting the timetable of trains for the remainder of today from Marshchapel Street Station.

Hilda gazed at him in exasperation. Would he never shut up? She was going to have to kill him and hide his body in the larder, she thought half-jokingly. Something stirred inside her; it had been a long time since she had attempted any killings. She took a quick gulp of tea. 'Not here Hilda, come on, get a grip', she told herself.

"You've got biscuit crumbs all down your front," she pointed out to Edwin, "Madame won't be too thrilled if she sees you in that condition."

"No, she won't, will she?" replied Edwin in a pleased voice.

The kitchen door opened and Edwin struggled to his feet as Madame entered.

"Not changed yet, Edwin?" she retorted.

Edwin pointed to the striped tie around his neck, and pulled a school cap from his jacket pocket.

"I am now Madame," he replied.

"Look at the state of you, you horrid boy. Get up those stairs now, and wait outside my door. And don't you dare drop crumbs on the stair carpet."

Edwin headed for the stairs at a fairly rapid trot brushing his hands down his shirt as he went.

Madame rolled her eyes heavenwards and looked at Hilda.

"You'd think he'd make a bit of effort at role play," she said, "was he all right in here?"

"He recited the timetable of trains due out today from the depot round the corner," replied Hilda, "another five minutes and I think I would have started screaming."

Madame grinned.

"Yes, trains are rather his thing. Sorry Hilda, I really should have warned you."

She turned on her heel and followed Edwin up to her study.

Chapter 12

"Hildegarde, put these on, would you please," Madame Tempest tapped on Hilda's door and stepped inside, carrying a bundle of clothes in her arms.

"Your white blouse will be fine. I need you to help me upstairs."

Hilda took the clothes and inspected them. There was a navy blue gymslip and a navy and gold striped tie.

"But I don't do this sort of thing, Madame. I don't like being hit. It's not my thing."

"Lewis fancies having a girl in class with him," replied Madame, "you just have to sit there *Hilda*, I won't be chastising you, and there will of course be a bonus in your pay packet."

"Certainly I'll be glad to participate Madame," Hilda could take a hint with the best of them, and the promise of extra payment sealed the decision for her.

Madame turned on her heel and headed up to her study. She was a tall, sturdy woman, and for this role play she had dressed herself in an academic gown. Hilda looked at her retreating back thinking that from this angle, Madame looked like a large, energetic bat.

Hilda popped the overlarge gymslip over her head. She knotted the school tie neatly under her collar before picking up the sash and winding it round her ample waist. Her fingers looped the sash expertly. It must be half a century since she had worn her grammar school gymslip, she reflected, but her fingers had worked on the sash as if it had been yesterday.

She opened her wardrobe door and gazed at the image in the mirror. She half expected to see a sexy St Trinian's style sixth former staring back at her. Instead she saw a dumpy elderly woman, wearing a school tunic which looked like a sack tied round the middle. She sighed and made her way upstairs, tapping on the door of the room which Madame had designated as her study cum school room.

There were two TV tables and chairs drawn up in front of the desk. Lewis, a bank teller in his adult life, was sitting at one of these tables diligently writing away in an exercise book. He was wearing short grey trousers, and sported a navy and gold tie which matched the one that Hilda had been given.

"Ah, Veronica," smiled Madame.

Hilda glanced behind her before realising that this was to be her role play name.

"Do sit down, we are discussing Masefield's poems."

Hilda sat and opened the exercise book which lay on the desk beside a photocopy of two poems.

The lesson started. Madame Tempest turned out to be a surprisingly good teacher. Hilda forgot her bizarre costume and took a keen interest in the subject. Lewis started to brat and was called out to Madame's desk for a mild spanking with the slipper. Hilda stared fixedly at the table top while he was dealt with before returning to his seat, a broad grin plastered across his features. Hilda felt slightly apprehensive despite Madame's assurances, she didn't want that to happen to her.

Madame set them a task writing their own versions of Masefield's Tall Ships poem. Hilda became totally engrossed, and the two hour slot which Lewis had booked passed by with startling rapidity. Madame Tempest collected their exercise books and corrected them while the two pupils finished off the session colouring in a picture of a tall sailing ship. Madame handed the books back. Hilda's effort had been rewarded with a gold star and the comment "very well done". Hilda gazed at the page, she felt inordinately proud of that gold star. A warm glow diffused through her body.

Hilda had scraped through her eleven plus examination and attended the local girls' grammar school where she had been in the bottom quarter of the lowest stream. She had just managed to pass five Ordinary Level GCE's, but the school hadn't encouraged her to stay on and attempt any Advanced Level examinations. Praise for good work at school had been very sparse indeed. Hilda glanced at Lewis's book. "Could do a lot better" was scrawled across his attempt. Hilda grinned. Maybe she could manage this type of role play for Madame after all.

Lewis was one of the favoured few who was allowed to take tea with Madame after the session. Hilda discovered him to be a gentle, quiet man, and she was completely at a loss as to the reasoning behind his brattish behaviour in class. He spoke one day about his days at "real" school. He had been a timid, bookish child, a natural target for bullies, especially the lads who excelled at sports. Lewis had been asthmatic and was often excused from football and cricket games. It hadn't been just the boys who had bullied him either, the Games master at his Public School had been particularly scathing of Lewis' feeble efforts when he did get on the sports field.

Lewis explained that he loved coming to "school" at Madame's because he could be a rebel, mess about in class and thoroughly enjoy himself carrying out the pranks he had been too scared to do as a boy. He worked in a bank, in quite a senior position, with lots of responsibility. Reverting to thirteen years old was, he said, a great safety valve for relieving his stressful life. It also helped his marriage he admitted. His wife tended to be something of a nag, one of these complaining women for whom nothing was ever right. After a session with Madame, Lewis found he was much more tolerant and amenable and could put up with her moaning without resorting to arguments. He did love her still, he said, it was just that sometimes he felt he could strangle her, and playing a schoolboy made him more charitable.

Hilda sat drinking her tea and listening to him. She wished that her murderous feeling could be assuaged so easily. She donned her gymslip quite happily these days, and took part in the lessons, but if it ever became necessary for her to use her garrotte on Lewis, she would do it in a heartbeat.

Chapter 13

Hilda was in her room, completely focused on her knitting. She was putting a cable pattern on the front of a cricket pullover, and she was trying not to drop any stitches from the transfer tools as she crossed them on the panel. A door banged upstairs, and Hilda heard Madame's voice.

"I'm not sure I want to do that, Rutherford!"

There was a muffled reply from Rutherford, followed by

"Yes well of course you would have to pay extra. A lot extra, probably double at the very least. And I don't think I have a suitable cupboard."

Intrigued, Hilda looped the transfer tools over the needles and went to lurk near the door where it was easier to eavesdrop on the conversation.

"You've got that big cupboard in the Dungeon, Ma'am, that would be ideal."

"I store things in it Rutherford. Things, not people."

"I really would like to try it," Rutherford replied wistfully.

"Why me, there are other people who do that sort of play. People with the proper facilities."

"Well I always come to you, Ma'am, I trust you."

"Oh Rutherford," Madame gave a deep sigh, "you've really put me on the spot. You'd better get downstairs and get changed. I'll think about it."

Hilda scuttled back to her machine and finished moving the stitches before knitting the row. She went out into the hall, ready to see Rutherford off the premises.

Rutherford, where had he got that name from she wondered. She had recognised him straightaway. His real name was Kieran Flynn, and he was a jobbing actor. She had seen him many times on the television, appearing in advertisements or playing minor supporting roles in kitchen sink dramas, usually as the working class side kick of the hero, a hard drinking, down to earth, no-nonsense character. His penchant with Madame Tempest was unknown to Hilda, she didn't follow the activities in the two playrooms too closely. He certainly wasn't into school role play, she knew that much.

As Rutherford left the premises Madame called to Hilda to come upstairs, and bring a tape measure with her. She was standing at the door of the Dungeon. Hilda had never been in that particular room before, Madame saw to the hoovering and dusting in there herself, along with the occasional help of a client named Wilfred. It was a fair sized room and she looked round curiously. There were a couple of stools, a St Andrews cross complete with shackles was placed against one wall, and a gymnasium horse took pride of place in the middle of the room. There were wooden and leather implements hanging from neat silvery hooks, a laundry basket crammed with canes of all shapes and sizes, a wheeled collapsible hospital trolley on which lay a nurses' uniform was pushed into one corner, and a large cupboard sat against the adjacent wall.

"I want to get this cupboard emptied, Hilda," said Madame Tempest, "then you can measure the base and get me a piece of foam from the upholsterer's in the High Street to fit in the bottom."

She opened the double doors as she spoke, and pulled out spare bedding which she placed on the top.

"See if you can get this into the airing cupboard will you." She bashed her fist on the underside of the shelf to see if it was loose. It rose up a couple of inches.

"We need to get this out too, and if you go to the hardware store you can get me a couple of bolts and a padlock."

"Yes, Madame."

Hilda was completely lost for words. Simple acquiescence seemed to be the order of the day.

Madame Tempest looked at her.

"I am so glad I kept you, Hilda, you make an excellent maid. Aren't you the teeniest bit curious?"

"I'm not too sure if I want to be curious," Hilda replied cautiously, "some of your gentlemen have some odd requests."

"Rutherford wants to wear a black rubber suit and be locked in the cupboard for several hours," replied Madame.

Hilda's jaw dropped.

"Why?"

"I don't know, I'm not a psychologist. It's what he wants and he's prepared to pay for it, so we'll go for it," she smiled cheerfully, "I carefully vet my gentlemen, Hilda. I admit they are all amiably eccentric, but I don't entertain the seriously weird."

Hilda looked at her employer who was bizarrely dressed in a black leather basque, fishnet stockings and long black soft leather boots with high stiletto heels. Hilda felt that her understanding of "weird" might not be the same as Madame's.

Also, she wasn't too sure about that "we". Hilda hoped her participation would end with the purchase of a foam mattress and a set of locks. At times like this she felt that she was living on a tightrope.

Despite Hilda's reservations, when it came to the first session, all went well, and having helped Madame Tempest to extract Rutherford from the cupboard after a four hour sojourn Hilda went off to make tea for the three of them.

They sat round the kitchen table as if they were three friends enjoying afternoon tea. Hilda was thankful to see that Rutherford was now dressed in his day clothes although his expression reminded her of the cat who had got all the cream. They sipped their drinks and indulged in small talk. Rutherford turned out to be a skillful raconteur. He recounted stories about out-takes and minor disasters during rehearsals and filming which had Hilda laughing out loud in appreciation. She found herself thoroughly enjoying herself, quite a novelty for Hilda Hopkins.

Chapter 14

Hilda settled easily into her new life. Her duties weren't onerous. Although she had to do the hoovering and dusting around most of the house as part of her maid's job, she did have time off, especially on the days when Wilfred turned up to role play a housemaid. It pleased Wilfred to strip naked, and work his way through the house, wearing a small, and to Hilda's mind, totally inadequate frilly apron while he scrubbed floors and cleaned paintwork to his heart's content. It certainly made life a lot easier for Hilda although she always made a point of doing something else while Wilfred was there. Usually she took her shopping trolley and pottered off down the High Street until he was due to be gone.

She dressed herself in her gymslip whenever Lewis booked a slot in Madame's study, and found that she secretly enjoyed the lessons. Her competitive streak kicked in and she strove hard to beat Lewis in tests and tasks. She still did not understand the reasons behind the men's needs but if it meant that she had a safe bolt hole she was quite happy to go along with the status quo.

Madame had upgraded her television set and generously she gave Hilda her old one. It had a built in DVD player, and Hilda loved it. She bought lots of DVD's from the local charity shop, and indulged her passion for action thrillers, horror flicks, and the odd comedy film. The romantic films she left on the shelf, Hilda liked a rip roaring storyline, preferably with a touch of humour in it. Together with her knitting machine, Hilda felt she was in seventh heaven. She could live like this forever.

Chapter 15

Hilda was busy in the kitchen setting the table with a plate of cakes, shop bought; Madame had sampled Hilda's baking and not found it up to scratch. Hilda had been aggrieved. She considered herself an excellent cook, but then, Madame did have odd tastes, look at the profession she was involved in. She flicked the switch down on the kettle and reached for the teabags. Madame would be calling any moment. Rutherford enjoyed his time in the bottom of the cupboard in the Dungeon, but he always needed help to stand up at the end of the session. His legs were just too shaky after being cramped in one position for so long. On a couple of occasions he had had to lie on the medical trolley while he got his bearings again. Madame had dressed up in her nurse's uniform to see to him, and Hilda had backed rapidly out of the room leaving them to whatever it was they got up to when they were alone.

"Hildegarde."

Hilda popped the last teabag into a cup and moved towards the door, removing her apron.

"Coming Madame."

Hilda toiled up the stairs and tapped on the half open door of the Dungeon. Madame was easing back the second of the bolts.

"Pass me the padlock key, it's on the stool over there."

Hilda obeyed, covering her mouth with her hand as she gave an enormous yawn. Perhaps she would have an early bedtime tonight she thought.

A gasp from Madame made her look up abruptly. All the colour had drained out of Doreen Morgan's face, leaving it chalk white. She had hold of Rutherford's shoulder and was roughly shaking him. The man lolled in the cupboard, limp and unresponsive.

'Oh no, not again,' thought Hilda resentfully, 'why is it always me?'

She crossed the room and bent down, unzipping the hood at the back of Rutherford's head. She pressed her fingers against his neck. There was no pulse.

"He's dead," she stated flatly.

Madame Tempest took a hasty step back.

"I told him it wasn't safe. I warned him. He would do it."

Hilda's mind had started to work. She slipped back into her old practice of plotting and planning with scarcely a pause.

"We have to dispose of the body, Madame, neither of us can afford to answer any questions regarding his death. This won't be a fine at the Magistrates' Court, it will be prison. Can you close this up for now?"

Madame obeyed, shoving Rutherford's body upright, and shooting the bolts back into place.

"I don't think there's enough air in there. It might have been that, he could have suffocated. He wanted a longer session this time. Perhaps I should leave it open."

Her hand went to the top bolt.

"He's dead," pointed out Hilda, "you can't kill him twice, leave it locked."

Madame's hand shot up to her mouth. She bit at her fingers, steadying herself.

"I didn't think. Come on Hilda, we need some bright ideas."

At least, thought Hilda, the woman was still in control of herself. Abigail Moffat had simply panicked when this had happened to her.

"Let's go downstairs, the tea's nearly ready. We'll have a drink and think about this calmly and carefully. Don't go off half cocked, that way lies disaster."

They sat opposite each other, drinking tea and eating cake. Madame could scarcely believe the incongruity of it all.

Hilda had both elbows on the table, and was holding her cup to her lips.

"Edwin!"

"What?" asked Madame, "we couldn't ask Edwin to help, he's useless at the best of times, and we don't want anyone else knowing about that."

She jerked her head in the direction of the Dungeon.

"Did you ever see a film called "The Ladykillers", one of those Ealing comedies?" continued Hilda as if Madame hadn't spoken.

"Erm, yes, years ago. Alistair Sim."

"It was Alec Guinness actually," replied Hilda, "he did an impression of Alastair Sim's method of acting, lots of people thought it was him it was so good."

"Hilda, what are you drivelling about?"

Hilda flushed, a wave of resentment washed over her.

"It's not drivel, do you want my help or not?"

Madame's shoulders slumped.

"Just tell me what to do."

"This film, it was a street a bit like this one. The men got rid of each other by dumping their bodies over the bridge onto trains. Edwin knows when the trains are due."

Madame still looked baffled.

"Can you get in touch with Edwin? Do you have his number or does he just ring here for an appointment?"

"I have all my gentlemen's numbers, it's a requirement. Real names, addresses, phone numbers, it's a sort of insurance."

"Do you ever give them written punishments, lines or whatever?"

Madame nodded.

"Can you tell Edwin you have a free slot, perhaps someone has cancelled, you make the excuse, you know what to say. Tell him he can come at a reduced rate, anything to tempt him here."

Madame frowned.

"I got the impression Edwin doesn't spend too much on role play uniforms, so he doesn't have that much money to chuck around?"

"True, but I'm not following you Hilda."

"Get him in, make him write out the time table of goods trains and passenger trains for the next two days in his best handwriting. Then whack him or whatever it is he likes and send him on his way."

Light was beginning to dawn.

"But how do we get Rutherford over the bridge. He's not a light weight."

'It shouldn't be that difficult,' thought Hilda, surveying her employer, the woman was at least twenty years younger than Hilda, and sturdily built.

"That hospital trolley of yours, the one on wheels, the one you do the Doctor and Nurses things with," Hilda's face creased in distaste, "if we get him onto that, we can roll him out into the street. Get Edwin to do a show and tell, find out which track the trains are likely to be on."

"What about Rutherford, what do we do with him for now?"

"Leave him where he is. He's not doing any harm. He's not likely to disturb anybody there now is he?"

Hilda smiled benignly at Madame. She shivered as the full force of Hilda's malevolence hit her.

Chapter 16

Edwin had arrived very promptly when summoned. He didn't seem to believe his good luck, an extra session and at a reduced rate.

"I thought I'd have to give Madame a miss this month," Edwin confided to Hilda, "Tramlines has to have her booster shots, and I didn't think I could afford both."

"What's Tramlines?"

"My cat. She's my only companion, and she's a beauty too."

"Ahh, right," murmured Hilda, "if you're ready, I'll take you up."

An hour later Edwin left the house, looking very pleased with himself. Madame Tempest brought down two sheets of paper covered in figures. The charts had been written out unexpectedly neatly, Hilda would never have guessed that Edwin's penmanship would be so precise. Her own handwriting was distinctly straggly.

Edwin had written out the times of the goods trains, and the tracks which they used, together with similar charts for the passenger trains. Hilda was pleased, this was ideal, they now knew exactly when a goods train could be expected to pass under the railway bridge. No hit and miss here, they had the precise times. That's what it took, Hilda thought complacently, careful planning, and no-one could surpass her at that. She felt omnipotent, the powers which ruled her were at full strength.

She bustled away to the kitchen and put the kettle on. Hilda needed a cup of tea to help her plan the next stage of disposing of Rutherford. Tea was the elixir of life for her.

"What we need now is a sheet of something like Formica, about six feet long and three feet or so wide." Hilda took another sip of her tea, "Something slippery. We can put Rutherford onto that then slide him off the trolley over the bridge into a truck on one of those goods trains."

Madame looked at her with respect,

"That would be easier than simply heaving him over the top," she conceded, "what gave you that idea, Hilda, have you done this before?"

"No. I was watching a film on the TV. That's how the Royal Navy disposed of their dead after a sea battle. Except they wrapped their dead in sails and sewed them up first before sliding them down this plank effort. We shan't bother doing that. The film's called HMS Defiant, it had Alec Guinness and Dirk Bogarde in it. You would probably have enjoyed it, Madame. Dirk Bogarde acted as one of the lieutenants, he was really evil, the acting was brilliant, and he took against the captain, and as the captain's son was on board as a midshipman, he had the lad caned every day for a week!"

Madame looked shocked.

"I don't have any connections with children or animals, Hilda," she retorted vehemently, "I have my standards, consenting adults over twenty-one only, nothing nasty like that. That is absolutely taboo in my book. I don't condone children being beaten at all, the idea is appalling."

Hilda swallowed more tea. She had badly miscalculated on that topic she realised.

"Of course, Madame," she said in a small voice, "I didn't mean to offend. But do remember, they had different standards in those days. We can't think of twenty-first century values when we are considering history."

"Just leave it, don't mention that sort of thing again, ever. We have got to sort out the problem that we do have. We need to get Rutherford out of here as soon as possible. There's a DIY place just past the park, drink up and we'll go across there and you can choose your piece of slippery wood. Did you check that timetable of Edwin's?"

"Yes, Ma'am. There's a goods train leaving the yard at 2315. It'll be dark by then. If we are properly prepared, we should get it done tonight."

Chapter 17

Hilda decided on a piece of work top with a shiny black surface. Less noticeable than white on a dark night she thought, but still slippery. They returned to Railway Cuttings and bumped the hospital trolley down the stairs. The piece of wood fitted on there perfectly. Hilda started to feel that this was going to work. Not that she had had many doubts, the planning was down to her, so they were bound to succeed.

The most difficult part was winkling Rutherford out of his makeshift tomb. Madame had recoiled when she saw the stains on the foam mattress beneath his body.

"Ignore it," hissed Hilda, "it's just natural seepage. We'll burn the foam once we get rid of him."

Both women were wearing thin vinyl gloves. Hilda was comfortable with hers, but Madame found the cloying plastic unpleasant on her skin. Hilda had taken a sheet out of the airing cupboard, and they eased the dead man's body onto this. They dragged him to the top of the stairs, then heaved him down, step by step. Hilda certainly couldn't have managed this one by herself. Even with Madame, who was relatively young and a strong sturdily built woman, it was a struggle to get him onto the trolley.

They had to wait until darkness fell. A few minutes before the goods train was due to pass under the bridge, Hilda opened the front door and looked up the road. Nothing stirred. The house opposite was in total darkness. Hilda looked back and gave Madame the thumbs up. The trolley was pushed out into the street in one strong smooth movement. Madame rolled it along the bridge almost as far as the signal gantry. This was the track which Edwin had stated would be used. Hilda hoped he was right.

Madame hauled on the trolley and lifted the front of the worktop so that it leant against the top of the parapet. Hilda pulled herself up until she was sitting on the edge and looked over the bridge. About six feet below her a pipe ran parallel with the bridge, passing behind the gantry and continuing on into the darkness. Not a smooth pipe, Hilda could see ridges along its surface every few feet. They would have to be sure that they cleared that with Rutherford's body. She could hear something. A train was approaching from the station, heading out, hopefully towards North Bridgechester and the power station.

"We need to push the worktop a bit farther out, there's a pipe down here, we don't want him getting caught on that."

She suited her actions to her words and helped Madame to push the work top a few more inches across the parapet, while holding tight to one side of Rutherford's corpse so that he wouldn't slip back off onto the road.

The engine chugged into view. It was still travelling quite slowly, and the two women could see that the tops of the trucks were open.

'Thank goodness for that,' thought Hilda, otherwise they would just be dumping the man onto the tracks. It would get rid of him, but they really wanted him to be found many miles away from here.

"One, two, three, now!" ordered Hilda

Madame lifted the bottom of the worktop sharply, Rutherford shot off the end, his momentum taking him clear of the pipe as he descended in a graceful arc and landed in a truck with a faint whoosh.

Hilda grabbed hold of the plank and nearly tumbled after him as she tried to stop it from falling over the parapet. Madame gripped it from her side, and angled it back towards the trolley.

"Come on", said Hilda, breathlessly, "let's get back inside. We need to clean up the cupboard."

They stumbled back into the hall, pushing the trolley in front of them. Hilda looked sharply at Madame. She looked green.

"You make the tea, and I'll clean out the cupboard." She gave her employer a small push, "go on, we'll leave this contraption down here until tomorrow," she patted the hospital trolley with her hand, "it's done Madame, we managed it perfectly. By the time they find him they will have no idea where he started out."

She smiled, and once again Madame Tempest felt the malevolence of the woman. She shuddered.

"Yes Hilda, I'll put the kettle on," she agreed as Hilda headed up the stairs.

Chapter 18

"Stop it, I don't like it! I can't take it! No more, please! You're hurting me, get off me you cruel bitch!"

Hilda Hopkins's head shot up. She was sitting just inside her bed sitting room, perusing a knitting machine magazine. The door was open as Madame had a client upstairs and it was Hilda's task to listen out in case of any complications. It was unusual to hear protestations, genuine ones that is, and these sounded real enough, but it was someone new up there. Stanley, he hadn't given a surname, had rung Madame's number and told Hilda that he wasn't local, he was staying in a hotel in London for a few days. He wanted to book an appointment, he said, explaining that he was down here attending a Pigeon Fanciers' convention, and being well away from home, he had decided to turn a fantasy into reality. From his shrieks of protest, it appeared that the fantasy was much more fulfilling than reality after all.

Hilda hovered by the door. Should she go up? But Madame hadn't called her, better stay down here, Madame wouldn't appreciate any interference in her dealings. A door banged and Madame shouted,

"Stanley, wait, dress yourself properly."

"I want my money back. I didn't expect it to be like this. It hurts," wailed the man, "you're evil. You want reporting, it's not anything like what I thought it would be."

Hilda hurried to the foot of the stairs just as Stanley appeared at the top. His trousers were down to his knees, and he was trying to pull them up. He teetered on the edge of the top step before crashing down the stairs. Hilda hopped back out of the way as he tumbled down gracelessly, arms and legs flailing in the air.

'Bloody hell,' she thought, Mr Lancaster had tumbled down the stairs at Travellers' Rest and broken his neck. That had started Hilda and Abigail on their murder spree. She looked down at the recumbent form on the floor by her feet. This one was breathing, although his leg was bent at a very odd angle, it looked like it might be broken. If it was, they would have to call an ambulance to the house. What would he say when he came round? Madame clattered down the stairs.

"He went all peculiar on me. Said he fancied a judicial caning. I didn't him hit that hard, I guessed he'd never tried any of this before despite him boasting he could take anything. I thought I'd warm him up gently but he started squealing like a stuck pig. What on earth did he expect," she gave him an exasperated poke with the toe of her long black boot, "of course it was going to hurt. It's punishment, it's meant to hurt."

"I think his leg is broken, Ma'am, we've got two choices. We ring 999, or else we put him out of his misery."

Madame sat down hard on the stairs.

"Oh no. We don't want the authorities round. But that, I don't think I can do that….." her voice trailed way.

"I can," replied Hilda coldly, "so long as I can rely on you to help me get him over the bridge? I've still got Edwin's timetable."

Madame bit her lip. She looked at the prone body. This wasn't one of her regulars, she didn't know the man, she wasn't going to miss him, and his relatives would have no idea who he was visiting down here. She let her breath out with a sigh, the decision made.

"Do it. Quickly, before he comes round. Wait, let me get back upstairs, I can't watch."

Hilda fetched a knitted cord and a stout knitting needle from her room.

'Like Madame said,' she thought, as she proceeded with "the business", 'you should have stuck to fantasy. It's not always good to get what you want, or what you think you want in this life.'

Madame had brought the old hospital trolley to the top of the stairs. She went down and helped Hilda to move the body to one side before she brought the trolley clattering down the stairs again.

"At this rate, Madame," muttered Hilda breathlessly, as they twisted the trolley to get it into the hall, "you ought to leave this frigging thing down here. It'll save a job getting it up and downstairs."

Madame shot her an irritated look.

"Profanity Hilda, I won't have it in the house!"

"Sorry Ma'am, I'm a bit stressed."

"And anyway, I'm not thinking of making a habit of this," Madame snapped petulantly, "if I had anyone else for a maid, I wouldn't have got away with the last one."

"No Ma'am, indeed you wouldn't", replied Hilda, with a wealth of meaning in her voice.

The nights were darker now, and colder. Hilda was thankful. It wouldn't do to drop the bodies into the same scheduled train each time, they needed a bit of variety for timings and destinations. She had no doubt that this, or something similar to this, would happen again. Hilda was a firm believer that everything happened in threes.

They had the process off to a fine art now. A few minutes before the train was due, they pushed the trolley along the pavement at the side of the parapet until they were a couple of feet from the signal gantry. Madame manhandled the plank onto the edge while Hilda kept the body steady, and seconds later they dropped it over the side. Madame peered over the top.

"Bulls-eye!" she reported. "He's on his way."

They pushed the trolley back indoors, and Hilda sat down to inspect the man's wallet.

"He really was a Stanley," she said, "Stanley Shufflebotham. Here's his ticket for the Pigeon Fanciers Convention."

She pulled banknotes from the wallet and handed them over to Madame. There were two credit cards. Hilda went through the wallet carefully but there was no sign of the pin numbers. Oh well, it might be as well to let Mr Shufflebotham just quietly disappear. Madame pushed two twenty pound notes across to Hilda,

"There you go, a bonus. Thanks Hilda, you really are a treasure."

'Just so long as you don't bury me, Madame', Hilda thought sourly as she picked up the money. "Oh, thank you Madame. I'm always happy to be of help."

Chapter 19

"I have a new client coming today, Hilda," said Madame Tempest. "I met him at that party I went to last Saturday. He will be using the name Timmy."

Hilda had been invited to go to the party with Madame as her dresser, but she had begged off. It was a BDSM party in an underground Dungeon at a pub and Hilda had just felt too squeamish about it. She had visited several Clubs with Madame, but this venue was just too small, Hilda wouldn't be able to find a quiet place to wait and avoid watching what went on. Madame had not been too pleased, but she appreciated that Hilda had genuine limits, so she left her at home and went off to the party with two of her professional friends.

Hilda had sat alone in the house in Railway Cuttings. She had wandered through to the kitchen to make a cup of tea, and sat moodily at the table contemplating her lot. The muted babble of the TV which she had left on in her room registered dimly on the edge of her consciousness.

Hilda sighed. She should be well content, she thought, so why this restlessness? She had a roof over her head, money in her pocket, lots of opportunities to knit, but she still felt on edge. She reckoned it might be the activities that went on here which were unsettling her. Despite an openness of mind, Hilda still found a lot of the practices here unnatural. This was a little odd, after all, Hilda had disposed of more than her fair share of victims by various forms of murder, but these, she thought dourly, were matters of expediency, not choice.

If she could pack up her knitting paraphernalia and disappear into the sunset she would do so. But where would she go, and more importantly, would Madame set the police on her? Madame of course was linked to a death, so maybe that would be enough to keep her quiet. But she knew so many influential people, Magistrates, Judges, solicitors, even high ranking policemen. A quiet word in the right ear could perhaps cut Hilda's career as a free woman drastically short.

'Count your blessings, Hilda', she told herself sternly, 'this will do very nicely for a few more months. Let's just see what the future brings.'

She realised that in essence what she was feeling was loneliness. At the Travellers' Rest Guesthouse she had spent many an afternoon or evening in the Guests' Lounge, with Abigail Moffat for company as the two women followed their hobbies, Hilda sewing up her knitting and Abigail indulging her love of intricate needlework. Madame was always in the house, but the two women never spent time together, other than at mealtimes.

She wondered briefly what Madame was doing now? She decided not to go down that road. It was bound to be something unspeakable. The kettle spluttered, clicked, and turned itself off. Hilda splashed water into a cup with a tea bag, added milk and carried her drink back into her room.

Chapter 20

Today was Monday, the beginning of another working week, and Madame had just told Hilda to expect a new client. Hilda knew most of Madame's special clientele by now, what was this one into, she wondered.

"Will he need to change first, do you know Madame?"

"Yes, show him where the dressing room is. He's bringing his own costume."

"School uniform?"

"No, he will be wearing pyjamas, pink ones if they are the same as the ones he was wearing on Saturday, with teddy bears."

"Of course," responded Hilda, "makes a nice change I suppose Madame."

Madame grinned.

"That's the spirit Hilda, variety is the spice of life you know."

She retreated up the stairs, and Hilda settled herself near the front door. Pink teddy bears, maybe he would be interested in buying a jumper. She could do any number of teddy bears in whatever shade of pink he preferred.

There was a loud banging on the front door as someone used the door knocker with unwonted enthusiasm. Hilda yanked the door open and stepped back to let the man who called himself Timmy enter.

'Timmy,' she thought, 'wasn't that the name of the dog in the Famous Five?'

The man entered the hallway and looked at Hilda expectantly.

"I've er got an appointment. I met Madame...."

"Yes, I know. Give me her tribute, then you can come this way and get changed before I take you up."

Hilda had averted her face, and the words tumbled out of her in a rush. She knew this man. He had been a guest at Traveller's Rest, one of the few who had returned a few times for a romantic weekend with his boyfriend. Abigail Moffat and Hilda had offered a discreet venue for people who needed to keep their romantic entanglements secret.

He had given Hilda his envelope together with a very searching look. Had he recognised her? For the moment he was keen to get changed, and slipped into the small room which Hilda indicated to remove his day clothes. As they went upstairs to Madame's playroom Hilda could feel his eyes on her. She tapped on the door and stood back to let him enter. Again he ran that appraising stare over her before stepping into the room.

He did know it was her. Hilda felt certain of the fact. What would he do? An anonymous tip to the police? He had no loyalty to Madame, he had only met her a few days previously. She felt the old stirrings deep inside her. It was time for the next killing. Hilda slipped downstairs and chose a cone of yarn. It was her favourite blend for this sort of thing, wool and nylon. She quickly threaded up her machine, set the Russell levers and began to knit a long cord. It took minutes. Timmy still had another forty-five minutes to go. Another forty-five minutes or so to live.......

He had left Madame's room and pounded downstairs looking distinctly satisfied. Hilda wasn't sure if that was the result of Madame's ministrations or anticipation of what he was going to do to unmask her. She looked at him, her face completely impassive.

"There's a cup of coffee for you in the kitchen. Madame likes to have feedback from her new clients, to make sure you got everything you wanted, perhaps make it better for next time" she explained. This wasn't true, Madame only ever invited her extra special clients to stay and have a drink after their session, but of course Timmy was unaware of this. Meekly he followed Hilda into the kitchen.

"Perhaps I ought to change first?" he said nervously, he was sure this was that woman. The one he had seen at Grimes Cove helping out in the Guesthouse. What to do? If he phoned the police he would lose his chance of having some fun here with Madame, he doubted she would carry on business for a while if she was raided and the woman, what was her name, Hilda something, Hopkins, that was it, if Hopkins was removed. She would probably get done for harbouring her or something. But she had killed a fair few people at that place, and she had already been on the run for some previous murders. Could he leave her free just so that his pleasure could continue?

"You look fine," she smiled. Timmy shivered; he could feel the malevolence rolling off the woman. Better sit down and have a drink, don't make her suspicious, she might make a run for it. He could ring the police once he was well out of the area.

In his agitation he swallowed half the coffee in one gulp. He was sipping the rest of the drink when Hilda excused herself and slipped out of the room.

She scuttled up the stairs. Madame was still in the playroom, putting it to rights.

"He knows me," said Hilda, "I've met him before, that Timmy, at the sea side. He used to bring his boyfriend to the guest house. He's recognised me, I can tell. He's in the kitchen now, drinking coffee."

Madame gazed at her.

"I had no idea. What are you going to do?"

"Use Edwin's timetable," Hilda nodded at the hospital trolley in the corner, "I told you we should leave that thing downstairs."

"I don't want to know!"

"I'll call you when I need the trolley. We'll have to wait until it's dark anyway."

Hilda returned downstairs, collected her garrotte and knitting needle and padded quietly into the kitchen.

Chapter 21

"Hello Simone, you all on your lonesome?" The club manager had paused by a table set for two in a corner of the room and was looking down at the young effeminate man sitting there watching the door.

Simon Owens, also known as Simone, turned in his chair.

"Oh hi Caleb. I'm waiting for Maurice, he's supposed to be meeting me here. He's the best part of thirty minutes late now."

"Not like him," replied Caleb thoughtfully, "maybe he's forgotten and is still in his flat?"

There was a chorus of shouts and cat calls behind them as the cabaret started. A large man in drag, with a distinct five o'clock shadow on his chin stood on the small stage, miming "Raindrops are falling on my head".

"I'll go round, see if he's there. Like you say, it's not like Maurice to dip out on an evening out."

The following morning Owens went to the police station to report his friend missing.

"What's his name," asked the Police Sergeant.

"Maurice Armstrong."

"Age?"

"Thirty-four."

The police sergeant sighed and gently explained that grown men often went missing without informing their friends or relatives. Did Mr Owens think that anything sinister could have happened to him? Maybe he should give Armstrong a chance to get in touch, leave it for a few days until he formally reported him missing.

"He's not likely to be too thrilled to find that half the police forces in the country are scouring the place for him if he's just gone off to recharge his batteries and get a change of scene for a few days now is he?"

Owens had agreed. He left the police Station and trailed forlornly down the road. It just wasn't like Maurice to up sticks and disappear like this. Owens had used the spare key to get into Maurice's bedroom and check the special shelf in his wardrobe. He left the flat feeling distinctly worried, there were only two pairs of pink pyjamas with the cheerful teddy bear pattern left on the shelf, there should be three. Owens checked the laundry basket and the washing machine. No third pair of pink pyjamas. Something was seriously wrong.

He felt he couldn't go back to the Police Station just yet. How would he explain the missing pyjamas? Would the police understand about fetishes?

Later that afternoon, he settled down at home for his evening meal. Tonight he would trawl round the gay clubs and bars in town, and see if he could find any trace of his friend. The TV was chattering away quietly in the background. He glanced across at it, the news was on. Owens watched as a picture of a train depot flashed onto the screen.

"The body was found in an open goods wagon at North Bridgechester. Tests are being carried out to see how long it had been there. The Police are appealing to anyone who knows of any persons, male, around thirty to forty years of age who may be missing. Unusually, the body had been dressed in a pair of pink patterned pyjamas." intoned the reporter.

Simon Owens let out a great keening wail.

"Nooooooo!"

Abandoning his meal, he rushed out, heading back to the Police Station.

Chapter 22

There was a tentative knock at the front door. Hilda went out into the hall, had she heard it or not? There came a louder, firmer rap on the wooden panels. Hilda slipped the chain onto its catch, and cautiously opened the door a crack.

Edwin was standing on the doorstep. What on earth was he doing here, Madame didn't have any appointments today so far as Hilda knew.

Edwin grinned nervously at her,

"I wondered if Madame had any freebies today?"

"You are supposed to ring for an appointment, Edwin, you know that."

"I've been watching the news. There were some interesting snippets, like those bodies turning up in goods train trucks........." Edwin trailed off and regarded Hilda intently through the gap in the door.

Hilda closed the door with a snap, removed the chain, and pulled it open.

"Don't stand there on the doorstep Edwin, you'll catch your death of cold in this weather. You'd best come in and I'll see if Madame can squeeze you in."

Edwin smirked and headed for the stairs.

"Not that way, come through to the kitchen while I speak to Madame. She may not be available."

She saw him safely into the kitchen and passed him a packet of ready salted crisps. Edwin accepted them greedily.

"I was at the Club the other Saturday. I heard Madame and Timmy chatting. I knew Timmy. Did you know he likes to wear pyjamas, pink ones especially? That last body they found had pink pyjamas. I was thinking about where they were all found, and all the trains must have started out from the yards at Marshchapel Street, it's a sort of common point."

He gazed innocently at Hilda out of limpid blue eyes. She felt like a rabbit caught in a car's headlights.

"I haven't got a clue what you are on about Edwin. Sit and eat your crisps while I see if Madame is free."

Hilda resisted the urge to make him a drink, she wanted him to be very thirsty in a little while. Hilda's mind was now working at full speed. She intended to give Edwin a special cup of coffee laced with valerian, but first she needed to be sure that Madame was ready to help her. If not, Hilda was quite prepared to take the handbag stuffed with banknotes and the small overnight case, which these days she kept packed ready for emergencies, and disappear over the horizon leaving Madame to sort Edwin out herself.

Madame was relaxing in her own room upstairs. She looked round enquiringly when Hilda tapped on the door and came in purposefully.

"We have a problem, Madame, a serious one. Edwin. He's downstairs in the kitchen."

"Edwin? Well I know he can be a nuisance but he's not what I would call a serious problem," grinned Madame, "is he reciting his train timetables again down there? Why on earth did you let him in, Hilda, he doesn't have an appointment today, this is my rest day."

"On the contrary Madame, he is very dangerous; his very simplicity puts us in peril. He knows that the bodies came from this vicinity, and he's put two and two together and made four out it. Did you know he was there on Saturday when you were playing with Timmy?"

"I wasn't playing with Timmy. I make it a rule never to play in public with any of my gentlemen," replied Madame, "Oh!!!"

She creased her face into a frown.

"I think I can guess. I was coming out of the loo, there's a sort of small lobby with male, female and disabled toilets coming off it, you know the sort of thing?"

Hilda nodded.

"Timmy was there, he asked me about appointments. And he wanted to play. I told him he could either play or make an appointment, so he said he'd ring but I told him to come along on Monday. There was someone else in the men's loos, I could hear them barging about, I suppose it could have been Edwin. He was at the party, and he was sulking because I wouldn't play with him, I remember."

"That certainly makes sense. We're going to have to get rid of him you know Madame. He's spiteful enough to go to the police if he's thwarted I think."

"I agree. Shame, but we have to look after ourselves Hilda. If we don't look out for each other, no-one else will. I suppose I can rely on you to do the er….gubbins?"

Hilda smiled coldly. Madame resisted the urge to shiver as she felt the malevolence emanating from the older woman.

"Let's give him a nice send off Madame. Can you see to him? Give him the sort of experience he likes? I want to lull him into a state of security, make him think he has us where he wants us. Once you've finished," Hilda's faced creased into distaste for a fleeting moment, "send him down for jammy dodgers and coffee. Edwin can't resist food, he's a greedy bugger."

"Language Hilda," Madame murmured automatically.

"Sorry Madame, I forgot, let's get it done."

As per Hilda's usual brilliance at arranging these things, the plan went beautifully. Several hours later Hilda gazed down at Edwin's recumbent form lying on the hospital trolley waiting for the 23:47 to North Bridgewater. It might have been nice just to be ordinary, she thought arrogantly, but the powers that controlled her had other ideas. If she was to be the best, it was only right that she should follow her destiny, and anything or anyone which threatened her would simply have to be eliminated.

She rifled through Edwin's pockets removing his wallet, and anything else she felt might identify him. She flicked the wallet open. There was a picture of a cat in there.

Edwin's cat, Tramlines. She had forgotten all about his beloved pet. Where would it be now? In Edwin's house, or did he let it wander? Probably locked in the house, he wasn't likely to let it roam off by itself when he wasn't there. Hilda frowned, she would have to tell Madame, they couldn't leave it to fend for itself. It was a pampered pet, it might not be able to cope alone, out in the wild.

Madame appeared, dressed in black, ready to blend into the shadows.

"Let's get it done, Hilda," she said, "the train will be along any minute," she gave a rueful smile, "we're getting quite proficient at this I think."

They suited the action to the words, tipping Edwin neatly over the parapet, and retired into the kitchen for a soothing cup of tea.

"I'm worried about Edwin's cat," said Hilda, pushing the open wallet across to Madame, "I wouldn't want it to starve or anything."

Madame looked at the picture.

"I've got a cat basket somewhere, one of my previous maids left it behind when she went. I think it's in the glory hole out the back. You're right Hilda, I don't like to think of an animal suffering. We'll go round to his house tomorrow and check that it's okay. It's the least we can do."

Hilda busied herself washing up the cups and replacing them in the wall unit. Her mind was working. If Edwin could track the bodies back to a common point would the police be able to do the same thing? Of course they didn't have the obsession with timetables which Edwin had had, and the bodies had turned up in different parts of the country, different police forces, but how long would it take before the link was made? Hilda decided she would update her overnight case and sort out a working capital too. She didn't want to be caught unawares; maybe she would buy a money belt and keep it with her all the time. Careful planning, she told herself, that's the key, keep one step ahead of the enemy at all times.

She glanced up as Madame came in from the glory hole, an outhouse in which all sorts of junk and unwanted items were stored, a cat box in her hand. And if she had to dispose of Madame to keep the other side at bay, well so be it.

Hilda gave her employer what she believed to be a friendly smile, it came out as a grimace.

"I'll say goodnight then, Madame, see you in the morning."

Chapter 23

Madame Tempest fitted Edwin's key into the front door and stepped inside, with Hilda close on her heels. Both women's noses wrinkled at the heavy musty smell in the place.

"Cats," murmured Hilda, "he mustn't clean the litter box out very often, or open his windows."

They went into the living room. A plate, half filled with uneaten food, was balanced on an arm of the settee, dregs of tea lurked in a cup which stood on the cushion next to the plate. The settee itself was partially covered in clothes and books which had spilled out onto the dusty, unhoovered carpet. The whole place was dirty and reeked of neglect.

They found the cat, Tramlines, locked in the kitchen. Hilda opened the fridge and took out a bottle of milk. She opened the top and gave the contents a cautious sniff. The milk was fresh. She offered the cat a saucer of milk which she drank greedily before sitting back and washing her face with a disdainful paw. She was a beautiful cat, sleek, jet black, well fed. Whatever Edwin's failings in the housekeeping department, he had certainly cared for his pet.

Madame produced the cat box which she had thoughtfully brought with her. It took them some time to get Tramlines into the box. She snarled and spat, and Hilda ended up with a nasty scratch down her arm, but eventually she was safely installed in there.

"Bloody thing," growled Hilda, running her arm under the tap. "You be thankful we didn't wring your neck or leave you here to starve. We are trying to do our best for you."

"Come on", hissed Madame, "let's get out of here before someone takes an interest in us."

She carried the cat box out to her car and dumped it on the back seat.

"There's a Cat Rescue Centre just over the river," she said, "I looked it up in the Yellow Pages, we'll take the thing there."

She waited impatiently while Hilda tugged her safety belt across her ample chest and buckled it in before setting off. Madame insisted on parking round the corner from the Centre, just in case there was any CCTV hereabouts.

Hilda picked up the box, and carried it into the reception area.

It's my neighbour's cat," Hilda had her story ready, "she's died and the cat's got nowhere to live. We can't keep it, we've got dogs."

She placed the box on the counter.

"It's young and healthy, needs a nice home."

The young woman at Reception smiled.

"It's very good of you to concern yourself with the welfare of the animal. So many don't bother, they would just leave it to stray."

Hilda gave a thin smile. The young woman reached for some paper work.

"I just need a few details. What's the cat's name?"

This took Hilda by surprise, she frowned. She hadn't expected to be asked that. Edwin had called the cat "Tramlines". This was an unusual name, would they be able to trace it back through a veterinary surgeon's records she wondered. Chances were that Edwin had kept the little beast injected with all the correct vaccines. She hoped he hadn't had her micro chipped, that really would put the fat in the fire. Hilda's neighbours had owned a cat, back in Merrydown Crescent, she had always been chasing it out of the front garden when it dug up the flowers. What was the wretched creature's name? Hilda's brow cleared.

"Snowball" replied Hilda.

The young woman gazed through the bars at the sleek, jet black cat now cowering in one corner of the box.

"Snowball, are you sure?"

"Yes," replied Hilda firmly, "she was a lovely lady, but eccentric, you know, liked to buck the system."

She looked at the clock on the wall.

"I have to go, the taxi will have its meter on. I just wanted to make sure that Snowball was safe."

She turned on her heel and scuttled out through the front entrance and back to Madame.

"Just drive, let's get out of here. The cat's safe, we've done our bit for Edwin."

Chapter 24

"So if I turn Queen's Evidence they can't do anything at all to me?" Hilda Hopkins froze. She had just entered number 6 Railway Cuttings carrying the weekly shopping. There weren't supposed to be any clients here today, so who was Madame talking to? And more importantly, what was she plotting? Hilda softly lowered her carrier bags to the floor.

She quietly eased the front door shut, holding the catch down until the last minute then carefully letting it click shut. Should she go closer to the kitchen? Perhaps not, she could hear quite clearly from here. Hilda had excellent hearing for her age. Moving around might alert Madame and her visitor to her presence.

"Nothing at all my dear Doreen, especially if I am there to direct the proceedings. If I'm not, I'll certainly use my influence to be sure that Counsel understands that you are in the clear."

"Thank you Tarquin."

Hilda jumped. She had thought she recognised the plummy tones of Tarquin Cressingham-Gore, but what on earth was the man doing here. He often came of course, he liked to role play as Matthews, a 1950's preparatory schoolboy, but Hilda knew there were no appointments for anyone today.

"You really have been a silly girl, Doreen," continued Cressingham-Gore, "have you no conception of how dangerous the Hopkins woman is? I must admit it took me some time to remember where I had seen her before. I could scarcely believe it myself when I did recall having her up before me."

"She just seemed so harmless at first," replied Madame Tempest, "I could hardly believe all that they said about her. She looks so inoffensive as a general rule. It was only after I had that little, er accident, and panicked that she came into her own."

'Which little accident was that one," wondered Hilda, 'Rutherford, Timmy, the Pigeon fancier or maybe Edwin?'

"Of course your name and er profession will have to come out in Court, and I doubt you will be able to carry on working here. The Police will want to keep a very close eye on any happenings in this house in future. But then, if you accept my proposition we will be able to continue having a bit of fun of our own. The flat I've got my eye on is in a very fashionable area, and I shan't object if you want to take a couple of your more affluent clients with you. It could defer expenses somewhat, my chick."

Hilda felt waves of rage flowing over her. She wanted to rush into the kitchen and attack them. She would kill both of them and heave them over the bridge onto the railway line. She breathed very deeply, feeling her shoulders come right up, before letting them slump again. Slowly she turned and eased the door open again and slipped outside. She walked down the short path and stood by the entry which separated the house from the railway bridge. The entry door was bolted on the inside; she couldn't slip down the side of the house that way. She slapped her hand down on the top of the parapet a couple of times. It hurt, and the action helped to steady her.

'Ok Hilda, let's get sorted. Back to your room and get your bits and pieces. Forewarned is forearmed.'

She returned to the front door and banged it open noisily, picking up the shopping bags as she strolled through to the kitchen.

"Oh," the surprise was feigned very nicely, "I'm so sorry Madame, I didn't realise you were expecting company."

She turned her eyes on the man sitting opposite to Madame.

"Matthews just dropped by, Hildegarde, to er…… to return a book I lent him. He's leaving now."

"Thank you Madame, I'll be in touch about the arrangements for that little matter. I think perhaps the sooner the better?" The question hung in the air.

"Yes, I suppose that would be best. Goodbye for now Matthews."

Madame turned towards Hilda and made a shooing motion with her hand.

"Very well Madame, I'll show him out."

Hilda bustled about, putting the shopping away and washing the cups which Madame and Matthews had left on the table.

It was late afternoon by now. Matthews had said he would put things in motion, Hilda could read between the lines, but it would probably happen tomorrow. Nothing was likely to happen tonight, especially if she kept Madame company as much as possible. Hilda checked her stock of valerian tablets. She would doctor Madame's coffee that would keep the woman quiet. How quiet, she wondered, should she polish her off? She sat at the kitchen table, a cup of tea in front of her. To do away with the woman, or not. What were the pros and cons?

Hilda sipped the tea, and felt the calming liquid moving down into her stomach. Madame would be soon missed. She had appointments on the morrow. Matthews, Cressingham-Gore or whatever his name was would certainly notice if she went absent. Then there was the simple practicality of getting rid of Madame's body. She was a tall sturdy woman, there was no way that Hilda would be able to raise her high enough to shove her over the parapet of the railway bridge. Hilda sighed. And of course, Madame had given her this job in the first place. Hilda had been quite comfortable here until now. Madame had even sussed out who Hilda was months ago, but she hadn't shopped her then, she'd let her continue living quietly in the house. As for turning Queen's Evidence, she was only doing what Hilda would have done in similar circumstances, looking after her own back, and letting anyone else go to the devil.

Hilda had checked her overnight bag. It had enough clothes in there to be going on with. She had transferred all her loose cash to the money belt that was sitting snugly around her waist. She had no intention of relinquishing that at any time until she was safely away from here. Would Cressingham-Gore wait until Madame had spilled the beans, or was he even now setting the wheels in motion?

Hilda busied herself making supper for the two of them. Nothing complicated, salmon paste sandwiches and slices of fruit cake. She brewed tea for herself and coffee for Madame, with an added ingredient of valerian. She indulged in small talk throughout the meal, striving very successfully to ensure that Madame had no idea that she was going to do a flit in the morning.

Hilda carried the dishes over to the sink and started washing them.

The telephone shrilled. Madame ran into the hall and snatched up the receiver. She listened for a few minutes, murmuring "yes" and "so soon" and "tonight" before adding "of course, I'll come now."

"I'm sorry Hilda, I can't do the drying up. I just have to pop along the road," called out Madame from the hall, "I won't be long, I feel tired out tonight for some reason." She checked that she had her mobile phone in her pocket and let herself out of the front door.

She was sorry she wasn't going to dry up? But, thought Hilda, Madame never did the washing up, or the drying, that was Hilda's job. What was she sorry about? Hilda shot across to the front window, she eased the lace curtain back and peered out. Madame was just climbing into a dark blue Bentley. Hilda recognised it, it belonged to Tarquin Cressingham-Gore, and it was his chauffeur who had assisted Madame into the car.

Hilda threw the tea towel down onto a handy chair and ran into her room. She dressed herself in dark trousers, and pulled on a navy blue jacket. Picking up her overnight case she cast a last look around her room. She paused only to stroke her knitting machine, this was the third one she'd lost, then resolutely she left the room and opened the front door, peering along the road to see if the Bentley had driven off.

It had, she looked towards the entrance of Railway Cuttings. The road was blocked, police cars were drawn across the street, and figures were starting to move towards this end of the road. Hilda rapidly retired back through the door, closing it quietly and slipping the bolts across. It was dark and gloomy down this end of Railway Cuttings, with a bit of luck her egress wouldn't have been noticed.

Chapter 25

"Police, Police, Police. Armed police. Stay where you are!"

Hilda Hopkins was already slipping out of the back door and into the side entry as the enforcer smashed into the front door. The entry door was locked at the street end, it would take them a few more minutes to break that in. She could hear activity in the next garden, the police must be swarming over the wall from that direction too.

Hilda climbed up onto the parapet of the railway bridge, and swung her legs over, groping with her toes to find the large wide pipe which straddled the railway line here. Carefully she let go with one hand and felt for the ridges on its surface which she knew were there. She let go with her other hand and let out a small "oof" as she thumped against the pipe. She was on all fours. She carefully inched her way forward, keeping her head well below the top of the wall. She could see the gantry ahead of her in the gloom. It seemed a lot farther away approaching it this way than it had when she had inspected it from the railway bridge outside number 6.

She was a fair way up from the ground. That didn't bother her too much, she had a good head for heights, but it was a long way down if she should slip. There were more cries behind her, and that leant wings to her flight, she scuttled forward towards the gantry, her eyes fixed on the ladder running down, she hoped, to ground level.

She was there. Her hands grasped the ladder, it was corroded and flakes of rust scattered as she grasped the rungs. Was it still used, she wondered? Well, she was using it now, she would soon find out. She hung on grimly as her feet scrabbled for a foothold, done it, she was on it securely. Just a matter of climbing down now. Hilda grinned, and stretched her foot down to the next rung.

She had only descended the first three rungs when she felt the Victorian ironwork in front of her start to loosen. There was a screeching noise as rivets started to pop out of the post holding it to the gantry. Hilda tried to scramble down more quickly but the top of the ladder parted company with the gantry and started to bend inexorably outwards.

Hilda could hear a train approaching. She was going to get hit by a train. It was all over. All her plans would end here with her body crumpled under tons of rail stock. She squealed out in panic and frustration. The ladder bent even further as a goods train thundered by beneath her. Her feet slipped off the rungs and her body swung backwards almost parallel with the track beneath her. She could no longer carry her own weight, her fingers lost their grip. Hilda screamed as she plummeted towards her doom.

Not quite her doom, she fell all of about eighteen inches and landed on her back, badly winded on a pile of gravel. Instinct had kept her head up, so she avoided banging that on the spiky chips. She lay on top of the gravel, arms and legs splayed out, looking like a frog pinned on a vivisection board. Her head fell to one side and she found she was breathing in the dust off the tiny chips of rock, it made her mouth dry and gritty. How long she lay there she had no idea, but eventually, painfully, she rolled over onto her front, knelt up, wincing as the gravel dug into her hands and knees, before twisting herself up into a sitting position.

She was free. Goodness knew where this train would take her, but Railway Cuttings and her career as a Domi-Knit-Rix were behind her. Hilda Hopkins was destined for pastures new.

Hilda Hopkins falls on her feet once again in *'Hilda Hopkins, For Queen And Country'*.